THE
CHANGING
TRAIL

THE CHANGING TRAIL

•

TRACY DUNHAM

AVALON BOOKS
THOMAS BOUREGY AND COMPANY, INC.
401 LAFAYETTE STREET
NEW YORK, NEW YORK 10003

PRINTED IN THE UNITED STATES OF AMERICA
ON ACID-FREE PAPER
BY HADDON CRAFTSMEN, BLOOMSBURG, PENNSYLVANIA

In gratitude to my parents, who taught me I could do anything, and to my husband, Paul, who believes the same thing.

Thanks, too, belong to Sherry Ebertshauser for rescuing me whenever the hard drive descends into chaos, and for being a good friend and fellow writer.

Chapter One

Higgh in the sky, the winter sun shone as though it were July on the frozen grasslands of the plains. Sparkling ice squinted the eyes of the Indians out hunting hungry rabbits. Snow balled in their horses' unshod hooves, forcing them to dismount regularly to pick the packed ice out with their knifes. The killing cold of the wind had died down temporarily, and the snow on top of the ice danced like the eyes of a young man courting a pretty girl. There'd been no rabbits, but the two hunters had time to pause and look around their stopping place for a second or two. Winter pinched their bellies, but this small stand of cottonwoods by a creek was pleasant, and there might be squaw wood they could take home to add to the fire. Eyes now on the ground close to them, the man on horseback and the one on foot were surprised to see a large lump covered with snow. Black tendrils of hair flowed from one end, and a hoof was clearly visible from the other.

"Dead horse," remarked the man on horseback.

"But where . . ." The voice of the man who'd been cleaning his horse's hoof faded as he knelt by the hump and swiped snow away from the horse's body.

"Hiyah!" cried the discoverer, tripping back so quickly he fell on his backside.

The Kansa who found the man and child weren't at all sure what should be done about them. Gutted, the horse had served as shelter for the pair. But the men who squatted at the corpse weren't at all sure if the two bodies curled in the frozen hide were worth saving, if they weren't already dead. Storms had raged for days, sheeting the plains with enough winter to send even the coyotes into their dens for a long sleep.

"Perhaps it would be a kindness to leave them," suggested the Kansa who, having dusted off his dignity, peered into the cavity. "When the thaw comes, we can come back and give them a proper burial."

"Humph," croaked the man on horseback. Icy winds rippled his horse's mane and sent cold through his boots. "Whatever we do, let's do it quickly."

Disturbing the dead was one thing, but leaving the living to die was another. The man at the horse's corpse reached into the guts with his bare hand and felt for warmth. Surprised at the faint heat, he gestured for his friend to descend.

"They may be alive. The animal hasn't been dead too long."

Quickly he felt the face of the child, Indian by the

looks of him, and then held his hand over the nose and mouth to feel for breath. The slight tremor against his palm sent him running for his horse.

"Give me your blanket!" he snapped to his friend. "The child lives."

Unsaddling their horses and jerking off the warm saddle blankets, the Kansa men knelt once more and pulled at the stiff arms of the black man clutching the child. Their tentative tugs did nothing to dislodge him.

"We'll have to cut his arms free, to get the child out," sighed the man who'd found them. He disliked intensely the idea of desecrating the dead.

"Then do it quickly," his friend urged. "No telling how much longer the child will live, like this." He gestured at the horse. "And I smell snow in the wind."

Startled, the man by the horse raised his head and sniffed the air. He'd been so absorbed in the two bodies, he hadn't noticed the shift in the wind's direction. Without hesitation, he slipped his hunting knife from its sheath, and began slicing through the frozen cloth covering the black man's arm.

The first cut through dark skin came too easily. Belatedly, he realized that a frozen corpse doesn't bleed. The red oozing from the wound proved them both mistaken about the black man. Swiftly he held his hand to the dark face, dusted white with a coating of frost, and felt, again, a soft breath.

"Help me!" he ordered, grabbing the man's legs and hauling. "He lives also!"

"I wish we'd stayed warm by our fires today," muttered his companion, grabbing a boot and pulling in tandem. "Trouble will come from this, just mark my words. Nothing but grief and trouble."

"How can you say that? Our wives will tend them, and if they die, we will bury them. Now help me!" Quickly he stripped off his jacket and threw it over the now exposed back of the black man whose bleeding arm still wrapped around the Indian child.

Seizing the child's body, he worked the boy free by hauling him under and out of the deathlike clasp. Quickly wrapping the small frame in his saddle blanket, he gestured for his friend to hold the boy. With a grunt, he knelt once more, and this time grabbing the man who was, after all, not so large, he hoisted the awkwardly bent shape over his shoulder. Jackknifing the body over the horse's back, he studied the issue of how to keep the twisted shape from falling. Nothing he thought of would work except for one.

Gingerly he stuck his boot in the stirrup iron and swung up behind the cantle. Without words, his friend, still cradling the small boy, tossed the other saddle blanket over the contorted man. Then he mounted beside him and reached for both sets of reins. Digging his fingers into the black man's hair and rump, his rescuer clicked at his horse.

"Gittup," he trilled in Kansa. "We must try to get home fast."

No telling how much longer the ice-bitten pair had to live, but neither of the Kansa men fancied hauling dead bodies to their families. They'd no food in their hunting pouches, but both sensed they'd bring either great trouble or the blessing of the gods into their lodges this day.

The winter of 1891 had been cruel to the real People, the Kansa who held the black man mused. Everyone had heard of the massacre of the Cheyenne at Wounded Knee. His tribe had long ago been decimated by disease and war with the whites. This black man and the Indian child would be his way of fighting that old demon, Death.

He didn't intend to lose.

Chapter Two

I am Mythmaker of the Kiowa, born Elizabeth McFarland, daughter of Colonel McFarland, sister to Noble McFarland, wife to Johnny Two Hats, mother of Whistle, and friend to Harry and Hannah Monroe. As I sit in the early spring sun and add to my collection of freckles, I am content.

"Mama, Mama!" Whistle, my four-year-old son, whose real name is John Noble McFarland Two Hats, rounds the corner of the house with his little legs flying, his dark hair standing behind him like a horse's roached mane.

I can't wait to see what new insect or snake he's brought for my inspection. A naturally curious child, he takes inordinate pleasure in the earth and its inhabitants. I swear, he has learned this reverence for the soil from Harry, a farmer who would rather ride his plow than the stars.

"Yes, dear," I answer patiently. Since returning from our months at the Kiowa-Comanche Reservation in Indian Territory, Whistle has had a tendency to cling to my skirts. I know Harry and Hannah have doted on him, and he seeks me out not from lack of love and affection. I have simply accepted the fact that there is a bond between us that, no matter how attenuated, pulls us together. Now that Whistle is out roaming on his sturdy little legs and under his own steam, he feels the need to reaffirm our connection at the oddest moments.

He lands with his balled fists in my lap, his pale eyes startling in his grubby face. This child will never be spit and polish, and I wonder, briefly, if he too would have disappointed my father, the West Pointer. Perhaps not. A grandchild holds little but delight for a grandfather. I could only wish my father still alive.

His tiny hands, already covered with ground-in dirt I don't believe will ever wash out, curl open to reveal a cocoon.

"I hold it verrrryyy gentle," he whispers. "Something lives, inside."

I smile at his perception, and at his mastery of English. Johnny had worried when, at two, he still spoke with his eyes and his tears. I'd soothed him by explaining that Whistle was hearing three languages at once, it would take him a while to sort them out. I was correct, and now Whistle chattered easily in his father's tongue, Comanche, my own, Kiowa, and English. Today he'd chosen to converse with me in English, but I never knew from moment to moment what language he would speak with me. A precocious child, he absorbs knowledge like desert heat sucks water. Hannah had begun teaching him his alphabet, and how to form letters with a stick in the dirt. I watched them together, the first few times Hannah answered one of his many questions and then showed him how to spell the word for the animal he'd quizzed her.

The tableau had taken me, faster than any train rattling across the prairie, back to my first years with the Kiowa. I'd taught Magpie, my adopted Kiowa son, his ABC's using the juice of berries for ink, hoping to prepare him for the day when he would lead his people and have to read treaties and understand them in English. My plans for him had gone awry, through no fault of my own. When I'd seen him last, just before Christmas of last year, he was an Episcopalian missionary who'd lost his vision. The Ghost Dance we'd danced together had given him something else, however. It had brought him into the world of Anna Jackson, the reservation schoolteacher. Her need for him gave him purpose once more.

I watched Whistle carefully fold his cocoon into my hand, and felt his residual warmth on the larva. His dark hair shone in the sun with a hint of red. This child, so curious, so vibrant, so eager to learn all the world had to teach him, was still a miracle to me. After Johnny and I had been separated for all the long years he was imprisoned at Fort Leavenworth, I'd never expected to see my husband alive again, much less bear his child.

In fact, I'd been told he had died in the penitentiary.

His return to me, at my brother Noble's farm, had been the beginning of a new life for us. We'd seesawed between the Reservation and life in the white man's world. I thought, after the massacre at Wounded Knee, we'd finally settled on life on this farm with Harry and Hannah Monroe as our final destination. But with my husband, I never knew what to expect.

I'd been compelled to return to the Reservation when the Eastern newspapers decried the Ghost Dance religion as another attempt by the tribes to massacre white people. Johnny had sought more than peace between our people; he'd searched for truth in this Ghost Dance. If the buffalo had returned and the earth had swallowed up all the white people, we would have been separated by death. I don't think he'd thought of that when he'd sought validation in the shuffling dancing that accompanied the plaintive prayers. To Johnny, I was Kiowa. Only when the white world intruded on our insular lives did he remember he too carried half-white blood by his soldier father.

I went to town more often these days, wearing my calico dress and bonnet. To the good people who saw us, Johnny and I were just plain folk. Johnny's lightly colored eyes hid his real heritage. For the sake of Whistle, I began to think in white terms more and more. We'd left the Reservation when I carried our son because we would have starved to death. We stayed away, to keep him from the Reservation's life of hopelessness and despair. And recently, I worried more and more about Whistle being labeled Indian. His education, his chances to succeed in the white man's world, would be irretrievably marred by his Comanche heritage. I thought now as a mother, not as one of the People, the only true People. When the time came, I wondered if I would warn him to hide his knowledge of our languages, our tales of creation, our sorrow at the death of the buffalo.

Sitting in the warm sun, I shivered at the knowledge of what I was going to do with our child. Johnny and I had never discussed his future. At the rate he was adding inches, we needed to determine *now* where Whistle would find his place in the world.

As though reading my mind, Hannah slipped through the doorway and found a place beside me on the bench.

"Sun kills a lady's complexion," she warned softly, lifting her own pale skin to the sky.

A light-haired woman, she'd been a prize catch for the Comanche warrior who'd taken her from this very farm. Harry had spent as many years searching for her as Johnny had passed in prison. She credited me with saving her life. In truth, she'd been my salvation.

"Fat lot we care," I mumbled, my eyes closed as I baked.

"If we ever want to be seen in society, we'd best start milk baths and cucumber rinses."

I peeked and saw that she, too, soaked in the spring sun like a hungry child sucks milk. "What's this about society?"

"I've been thinking," Hannah began cheerily enough, her voice a trill.

I groaned. "Not again. What will Harry say this time?"

She patted my leg, forcing me to pay attention to her. "This is important. It's about Whistle."

The five of us had had no disagreements, except for that one time. Johnny and I had wanted Whistle to return with us to the Reservation to see his People, but Hannah and Harry had insisted he stay with them. As it turned out, they'd been right. Johnny and I had had enough to contend with, without adding worry for a small child's safety from Army guns.

I sat up and, shielding my eyes with my hand, squinted at her. The years had been as kind to her as to me, and though our hair and looks faded, we knew each other well enough to speak our hearts.

"What about Whistle?" I tried unsuccessfully to keep the edge from my voice.

"He's growing fast." She gave me a look that said I was derelict for not noticing this fact about my child.

"Of course he is. He eats like a horse."

"No, not that." Hannah frowned. "His mind. He's quick, Elizabeth. I've never seen a child learn so much so easily. He has an ability most adults would envy. A natural-born learner. What do you plan to do about it?"

I knew Hannah already had something up her sleeve, but to give her credit, she was at least going through the motions of deferring to me, Whistle's mother.

"Thought we'd keep on teaching him, here at home. Both of us are educated women, Hannah. Johnny and

Harry can give him the things boys learn from men.''
I spoke cautiously.

''That's not enough.'' Her response was so quick,
I knew I'd been correct in my assumption she had
planned this attack carefully.

I sighed. ''Spit it out, woman. What's brewing in
that mind?''

''He needs to go away to school. A real boarding
school for boys. Not that place they set up for Indians
in Virginia, but a college preparatory school. Like
Christ Church.''

''He's only four years old!'' I screeched. ''And
you're planning to send him away? How are we going
to pay for this, may I ask? And what about him? How
does a child grow up without parents to guide him?''
I had the Indian abhorrence of taking a child from the
home. A visit to relatives in another tribe was one
thing, but a long-term severance of the parent-child
relationship was impossible to imagine.

''Not too early to start looking, see which school
we think would serve Whistle best. I'd like to see him
at Dartmouth, but perhaps Yale.'' Hannah ignored my
protests.

''And as to paying for it, well, I have the money
from Mama's house. Invested properly, it should do
the trick. Plus . . .'' Hannah plowed on ahead, ignoring
the impatient tapping of my toe in the dirt.

''Plus, we could take a house near his school.
You and I. The men will visit us, when time and the
crops allow. So you see, Whistle will be near family,
and—''

"And you'll be free of this place." I waved my arm, gesturing at the rolling land planted with wheat.

"No, I meant to say, and you will be free of this place." Hannah deftly turned the tables on me.

"But I have no desire . . ." I let my thoughts wander away from Kansas. Once, a lifetime ago, I'd been a student at a ladies' seminary in Virginia. The green hills of the Roanoke Valley had been home, until I'd grown to love the wide skies and sun-drenched earth of my husband's homeland. Somewhere within me was a corner that longed to see the dogwoods in bloom, a riot of azaleas in full blaze of color.

"I will not leave my husband." I shoved all thoughts of the East away.

"You won't be leaving him. It's only for a few months of the year, and only until Whistle is a little older, and can ride the train by himself." Hannah was matter-of-fact.

"I can't take your money from your mother's estate. It's not fair to Harry, for one thing. And I've no way of repaying you." Stubbornly I crossed my arms and again shut my eyes.

"It's not a loan. It's a gift. And Harry doesn't want anything from my mother's money. He has all he wants, right here." Her blue eyes stared at the land. Her husband's affection for dirt rivaled only his own for her.

"We'll talk about this later. When he's older. Like, sixteen." I tried to sound final.

"No, that's too late. He'll be so far behind, he'll never get into a good school. We need to move now, while he's young and eager to learn. I've written for information from several boarding schools, and I thought we'd take the train, ride East, see what we think.''

I'd faced the United States Cavalry, howitzers, and capture. But nothing in my life had prepared me for the irresistible force that was Hannah Monroe.

I gave protest one more try. ''We can't go now, it's spring planting.''

''Almost over with. There'll be some slack time coming up, the next few weeks. Perfect time for us to take off.''

I gave up. ''Is Whistle coming with us?'' I should have known better than to ask.

''Of course. We want him to see these schools. And for them to see him.''

I knew what she was really saying. She wanted them to see Whistle, and gauge their reactions to his hybrid looks. Remembering my girlhood in boarding schools as my soldier father fought first the Confederacy, then Indians, I had to admit my upbringing could have been much worse. Still, nothing I'd learned in the East had prepared me for my capture by the Kiowa. But those days were long gone. No tribes roamed the prairies at will, killing and taking what they wanted from any and all.

''He's still too young,'' I protested feebly once more.

''He's wise beyond his years. And with the proper education and background, he can go far.'' Hannah rose, dusting off her black skirt. "I'll tell the men, tonight, that we'll leave as soon as we can pack."

I bowed to a superior force and let her carry me down the river of this scheme. A visit back East didn't necessarily mean compliance with Hannah's plans. And I did want Whistle to be with more children, to see other places.

"A short visit," I warned, standing also. "And we come home whenever I say so." I knew I couldn't stand being away from Johnny very long.

"Of course," Hannah said and grinned. "Whatever you say, dear."

I mentally shivered. I knew Hannah well enough to know that *that* look meant I was doomed to go along with her.

But would my husband?

Chapter Three

‘‘We need to go to town,’’ Rebecca McFarland ordered her husband. ‘‘Nothing you can do to make the wheat grow, staring at it, and we could use a change of scenery.’’

Noble peered at his redheaded wife over the saw he was using to cut floorboards for the small shanty. The older boys had reached the age where they needed more space for their long legs, and they'd decided to let them move into the tiny house he'd built years ago for his sister, Elizabeth. She'd left suddenly one day, when her half-Comanche husband had come back from the dead to claim her, and they'd heard nothing since. Rebecca knew he still thought of her often, when she'd see his eyes wander to the shanty.

‘‘Work to be done here,’’ Noble said with a grumble.

‘‘Always work around a farm. Now go wash up. I'll

have Sam hitch the wagon. I feel like a sarsaparilla.''
Turning on her heel, Rebecca marched from the barn
with the assurance of a woman who knew she'd be
obeyed. Their years together had been long and fruit-
ful, with a houseful of children, one already grown
and married. They'd also come to an early agreement,
not long after Noble had returned to her after giving
up on talking his sister into leaving the Kiowa she'd
adopted as her own. Their first farm had been
Rebecca's, and she let Noble know in no uncertain
terms that she'd have equal say in how their land and
their lives were guided. But sometimes a woman had
to have her own way, and Noble understood that
completely.

Today was one of those days. Spring planting was
finished, and Noble and the boys had plowed under
more acreage than ever. She was tired of feeling like
a widow to the land, and even though no longer in her
first youth, she wanted a day with her husband when
he wasn't worrying about the quality of seed or if the
second plow would hold up another season. Taking
him to town was her only defense against a farmer's
constant worry for his crops.

Pinning on her good black hat, Rebecca tugged at
the tight cuffs of her blouse and made sure she looked
town-ready. The children, already primed by her earlier, had washed hands and faces and stood ready to
spend their Christmas nickels at the general store.

''Marianne, hold onto Edith when we get to town.
Jeremiah, make sure the picnic basket makes it into
the wagon.''

The children mumbled their ''yes, ma'ams'' and shifted anxiously as they waited for their eldest brother to bring the wagon to the front porch.

Rebecca checked the watch pinned to her bodice. Impatient, she tapped her boot on the braided rug in her front room. When no boots crossed the porch, she gave up any pretense of decorum.

Marching outside, she stood, arms akimbo, on the top step, and shouted, ''You come now, Noble Mc-Farland, or I'm going to town without you, and I intend on spending every last dime we have!''

Grinning, Noble drove the team out of the barn as Eli shut the doors behind him. ''Hold your horses, woman. Had to find my Sunday hat.''

Giving her a wink that said he'd been pulling her leg in keeping her waiting, Noble sprang down to help his wife up onto the seat. ''Still the prettiest woman in Kansas,'' he whispered as she gave him a half-annoyed, half-forgiving look.

''Not hardly. But I'll be a much happier one after I do some shopping.'' She waited until the children had piled in the wagon bed, before pushing up her umbrella.

Noble raised his eyebrows at the umbrella. ''Not Sunday, is it? Know you wouldn't have let us miss church.''

''No, but I'm wearing my good hat, and I don't want the sun to fade it.''

Noble chuckled, knowing she was getting more vain about her freckles as she grew older. He happened to love every one of the splotches, but Rebecca, her hair still a dark red despite being almost a grandmother and older than he, was beginning to rail at the signs of age. He'd been eighteen when the buffalo hiders had bushwhacked him and left him for dead. She'd saved his life then, and in the many years since, he'd thanked God for seeing that she was the one who'd pulled him back from the grave's edge. If she wanted to carry a parasol on a perfectly beautiful spring day, he'd not say another word about it.

They rode in to Larned, stopping to eat the fried chicken and biscuits Rebecca had packed as though it were a holiday. Noble had to admit, he'd been pre-occupied recently with the spring planting. He'd bought a few more acres last fall, planning on parceling them out to the first of his boys to marry. His daughter Elizabeth, named for his sister, was already settled on her husband's land nearby. Having been raised in the Army, Noble wondered if his children realized how blessed they were to live all their lives near kinfolk, to be able to count on family in times of need.

He still marvelled at his brood of children, and how each one seemed to fit into the life of a farmer with unspoken ease. Rebecca, the farmer long before he'd given up scouting for the Army, must have been the one responsible for the sensible side of their souls, not him.

Larned had changed much since the days when it was a stopping place for those heading farther west on the Santa Fe Trail. Built near the Army post of the same name, it had supplied immigrants with seed and plows for a long time now. But over twenty years had passed since it was a stopping-off place for sodbusters, and in 1891, it boasted a confectionery and more shops for gee-gaws than he would have thought possible. Pulling up at the livery, where he intended on leaving the livestock until Rebecca got her wild oats sown, he remembered how he would come to town to buy foolscap and ink for his sister. Wearing her black widow's weeds, she would sit at a rickety table, precariously perched in the tall grass, writing. Hours would go by, and he'd peep at her as he finished his chores in the barn, and her hand would still be flying over those sheaves of paper. He'd often wondered what she'd wanted so desperately to commit to those pages, but he'd never had the nerve to ask. He and Elizabeth hadn't spoken the same language since he'd found her in the camps of the Kiowa with his best friend, Johnny Two Hats, planning a life together with the tribe.

Shaking off the memory, he wondered why, of all days, his mind kept coming back to Elizabeth. His wife was ready to unload some of their hard-earned cash in the palms of any merchant with a pleasant manner and decent dry goods, he should have been worried about that.

''Think I'll save the sarsaparilla until later. Meet me at the confectionery around three o'clock?'' Rebecca gathered her girls around her, shooing the boys to him. ''We're going to start with ribbons and other female things. I'll get the boys from you after we have our treat, and take them shopping next. Matthew, try to stay out of the horse troughs, and if those short boots still hurt, that's too bad. You have to wear them until I can get you a new pair this afternoon.''

Their nine-year-old son hung his head and scuffed the dirt with a wince. How did mothers always know what a boy was thinking before he knew himself?

Noble laughed, sensing a flurry of patterns and new fabric spread on their bed tomorrow, as Rebecca and their three older girls planned new dresses. Baby Edith, their youngest, clung to Marianne's hand, as ordered. ''Just remember, I've got taxes to pay on the land one of these days,'' he quipped as Rebecca turned with her entourage to begin her assault on the mercantile.

''Hmpfh,'' she tossed over her shoulder.

He decided to start with his sons at the gunsmith's. The boys had used the old shotgun to scare crows from their fields for so long, they'd turned into pretty good shots. Matthew, at seventeen, was long overdue for his own hunting rifle. He'd check out the prices, let Matthew heft a few to see which he preferred, and think about it as a birthday gift.

Spring that year had been late. He'd held off planting until the last minute, afraid of crop rot. But so far, the new shoots looked healthy, and the soil was rich from all the rain, so he could afford to be generous with his children, he thought. He was a happy man, and he knew it. If only his sister had come to her senses and not thrown everything away on her half-breed husband and his people, he would have known he'd been blessed.

The commotion in front of the gunsmithy stopped

him in his tracks. Random gunplay had long ago been driven out of Larned by the law, but a man with sons couldn't be too careful. The sun reflected off the smith's window, temporarily blinding him as he held a restraining hand on Matthew's and Eli's shoulders.

"Don't want to get into something we can't get out of," he warned, listening for the tone of the voices.

But all he heard was excitement, not danger. The crowd gathered in the street buzzed for a few seconds, then Noble could hear someone shouting that the doc was out of town, had been for a few days, called away on some case. Noble knew what he had to do. Rebecca had been midwife and healer in the early days of her widowhood, setting broken bones, prying out spent bullets. If there was a need, she could still roll back her sleeves and doctor.

"Anyone need help?" he called from a safe distance.

"Man here, these Injuns say needs some. Looks like they done their best for him, but he's lacking some parts."

"Matthew, go fetch your mother. Tell her someone needs her doctorin'." Noble ordered his other sons to stay put, a command he knew they wouldn't obey, as he elbowed his way to the front of the crowd.

They'd brought the man in on a litter, dragged behind a horse. The scruffy bay's tail swished at flies, saving the dark man in the travois the bother. When he raised his hand to shade his eyes, however, Noble saw that he'd lost most of his fingers on the left.

"What can we do for you, mister?" Noble squatted

beside the travois, getting a closer look. The man seemed to him to be mostly black, with some Indian in there somewhere. Looked right peaked, though.

"Let me die," the man said, snarling. "Just make sure them Kansa get the boy to Indian Territory. Woman there, she'll take him in, raise him right."

Noble glanced at the crowd, searching for any sign of a black child. Dismounting, one of the Kansa abandoned his stony silence and hunkered down beside Noble.

"Boy with him when we found them. Little over three moons ago. Boy speaks no English."

Noble followed his eyes to the Indian child perched on the saddle on the horse this speaker had been riding. Tadpole, Noble thought. And definitely not this man's child.

"How sick are you? What's the problem?" Noble squinted at the man. He appeared thin and weak, more than anything else. "No sense talking 'bout dyin', if there's no need."

The Kansa spoke before the black man could. "Found them in the blizzard. Had to cut off some toes, some fingers. Kept the dark sickness from his veins. Thought he would get well. But a few days ago, he starts spitting blood. We won't have the lung sickness in our lodge."

Noble understood. They feared he had tuberculosis. Quickly Noble pressed his palm to the black man's forehead. He was somewhat warm, he thought, but nothing that warranted alarm. He wished Rebecca would hurry up. Strangely he felt responsible for this

specimen of humanity, and he didn't know why. He'd
seen some of the folks who'd caught the consumption,
but it seemed to him they coughed their innards out.
This man looked to him to be mighty weak and probably not too thrilled to have lost his trigger finger if
he was a lefty, but he hadn't set his foot on death's
door, not yet.

Sensing the crowd beside him shifting, Noble pivoted to search for his wife. Her umbrella forgotten in
the urgency of his request, she elbowed her way
through the curious like a woman on a mission. Seeing
him, she quickly dropped to her knees beside him.

"What is it?" Her eyes never left the dark-skinned
man on the litter. "Gunshot?"

Noble touched her arm gently. "Not so bad as I
thought at first. Got frostbit, back in the big blizzard.
These Kansa"—he nodded at the man still squatting
beside him—"evidently took him and the boy in. Did
their best with the fingers and toes, but now he's
coughing blood."

Rebecca echoed Noble, laying her strong fingers
against the man's cheek, down his neck to his pulse.

"Slight fever. I'd say it's more malnutrition than
anything else. That, and he never had much chance to
recover from the frostbite. Might have pneumonia.
Have the boys bring the wagon around, Noble."

Noble turned to find Matthew behind him. "You
heard your mother. Gather up the rest of the family,
while you're at it."

Matthew's eyes, round as windmills, stared at the
black man with a tangle of long hair and ragged shirt,

then at his father. He knew better than to question his parent at a moment like this. He ran for the livery.

The black man grabbed Rebecca's wrist, his hand with its missing fingers no oddity in ranching country, where a careless rope and a pommel could slice off a digit like a knife.

"Don't want no charity, lady. Just leave me, take the boy. White woman I know in Indian Territory, name of Mythmaker, she'll take him on. She done raised one Indian child I know of, already. He turned out all right, figure she'll do the same for this one."

Noble's heart hit his ribs like a hammer on an anvil.

"What did you say?" He sounded harsher than he intended. Rebecca clutched his forearm in warning.

"Her name's Mythmaker. Married to a half-Comanche, called Johnny Two Hats. Tell her the boy's name is Feather." The black man refused to let go of Rebecca's hand.

"Tell me you will, mister. Get the boy to her. Don't want him sold to some dirt farmer for cheap help. You hear me, mister?" The man's voice rose like the wind before a tornado. "Promise me. Don't leave him with these Kansa. He deserves a chance!"

Prying her hand loose, Rebecca swung to her feet. The crowd parted as she first searched for, then found, the boy who had the ill man so upset. Without a word to her husband, she pulled the boy down from the saddle and carried him over to the travois.

"This the child?" Her voice was gentle.

"Yes, tell her his name's Feather."

"I will." Rebecca placed the boy on the ground

beside her and held his grubby hand as though it were the most natural thing in the world for her to take on another responsibility. "Now be easy, stranger. My boys will be here with the wagon in a few minutes, and we'll have you into a clean bed in a tick."

The black man's eyes slipped shut, and his breathing seemed to ease. Noble knew he couldn't stand. How did this man know his sister? Was she really in Indian Territory after all these years? She'd left with Johnny when Rebecca was pregnant with Edith, and Edith was five now. There'd been nary a word from her in all this time, and in his mind, she was dead. Or as good as.

"Noble!" Rebecca's voice had an edge to it she rarely used.

Glancing up, he saw the wagon, with Matt holding the leads, the children already loaded. Awkwardly he pulled himself up from his squat and stared at the travois.

"Help me get him loaded," Rebecca commanded. She'd already handed the Indian child to Marianne.

He wondered how long he'd been staring at the black man, not seeing him, but his sister. He'd often imagined how she'd looked the day she'd slipped away from the farm before dawn, leaving her black dress and all her white clothing neatly folded on her small bed. Elizabeth, his eldest, said she must have worn the Indian garb she'd saved all those years she'd mourned for Johnny. Did she still dress in leather and beads? He couldn't see her that way, try as hard as he might. To him, she was always the blond-haired girl who'd been more a mother than a sister to him, having been the one in charge after their mother died and their father was off soldiering.

"Noble McFarland, quit your wool-gathering and get his knees." Rebecca was all business. "Matt, you take his shoulders, and I'll get the back of the wagon down."

Still in a fog of images of the sister he'd forced from his mind, the sister who'd betrayed her own race and chosen to live among the Indians like a savage, the sister with the finishing school education and the good breeding of a McFarland, Noble obeyed his wife. Rebecca placed the boy in the wagon bed, next to the invalid, and climbed up beside them.

"Take it easy on the way home," Rebecca ordered as their children stared at the strange pair in the wagon bed.

"Mama, that man's *black,*" Jeremiah whispered, as though no one but she could hear him.

"Well, God made us with infinite variety, son. What's your point?" Rebecca was busy inspecting the child for signs of illness, grateful that he seemed healthy, although thin.

"What will we tell people about him?" Jeremiah was at that awkward age when how he appeared to his friends was more important than food or sleep.

"Not a blamed thing," Noble snapped. "None of their business. Your mother's saved many a hurt critter, including your pa. Just do as she says, and no questions asked, son. You understand?"

Rebecca stared at her husband's back with a soft

light in her eyes. She didn't know what would happen with the child, and if he'd go looking for his sister, or not. But she'd do her best to make sure the black man lived, and maybe, he'd tell them about Noble's sister.

She'd been praying for this day since Mythmaker had left their farm. She'd never expected a black man found by the Kansa in a blizzard to be the bearer of the news she'd sought. But she'd long since given up trying to unravel God's wisdom. Smiling at her children, she tried to reassure their concerned faces that they hadn't brought the plagues of Egypt into their lives.

No, far from it. This black man and his Indian child were the key to healing for her husband, and she was grateful to God for sending them to Fort Larned, Kansas, on this beautiful spring day.

Chapter Four

‘‘He could go to school in Saint Louis.’’ Hannah was packing.

I watched her folding clothes into neat piles, sorting them as though arranging the order of our lives into shirts, petticoats, and frivolities.

‘‘You should buy a red dress when we get there. You'd look pretty in red,’’ she suggested by way of a peace offering.

‘‘I looked awful in red when I was a girl. I'm certainly too old to wear it now,’’ I countered.

I still wasn't sure about this trip. But Hannah was determined, and I was amazed at how Harry and Johnny seemed to fall into line with her. Hannah's power was immense. It was a good thing she didn't abuse it regularly, I mused as I hauled the carpetbags closer to the bed.

We still hadn't decided if one of the men would

accompany us. I didn't feel the need, but I knew Hannah would be happier with her husband along to handle the luggage and the hotels. Harry, during his long years of searching for his beloved wife, had hardened into a man who could get anything done, no matter what the price to himself. He'd do whatever Hannah wanted, except leave his beloved land. I knew how he felt.

While the Ghost Dance and its aftermath had sapped much of my happiness at seeing my people, the Kiowa, I would find it hard to know I could never see them again. Harry felt that way about his crops. It was the only bone of contention between Harry and his wife, but it stuck in the craw of each. Hannah, I believed, hoped that Harry would find something closer to civilization he would be happy with. Perhaps he would, but I didn't believe so. If I'd learned anything about men in the time I'd been married to Johnny, it was that they never changed. They loved, they cherished, they would die for their families. But change was another issue altogether.

"He'll go to school where Johnny and I agree he will go to school, and you know that, Hannah Monroe, so stop all this"—I searched for an inoffensive word—"planning. We can spend some time in Saint Louis, and if there's something appropriate for Whistle, I'll discuss it with his father."

I was having a hard time keeping Hannah's enthusiasm from running away with her. She was so happy to get away from the farm for what she hoped was the last time, I wasn't sure she'd come home when I wanted to leave. But I'd face that moment when it came. I'd agreed to this plan, I'd ride it out.

"Let me have the smaller one. I'll put Whistle's clothes in it."

Shooting me a grateful smile, Hannah passed me the small pile she'd laid on the quilted bed top. The object of all this attention hurtled into Hannah's bedroom with all the force of a deer escaping a hunter's sights.

"Mama, Mama," he shouted, and then he continued in Kiowa, "Papa says to tell you Uncle Harry will take us tomorrow, and to hurry, he has some things to say to you. He's in the barn."

"English, Whistle," Hannah chided.

"Tell Papa I'll be there in a minute," I answered in Kiowa.

I waited until Whistle had galloped back outside. I still thought he was too young to worry about his education, but Hannah was right, he would soon need companions his own age. I wondered briefly about my brother's brood. His youngest would be close to five years old by now.

"Hannah, the child can speak three languages, which isn't an easy feat for an adult. You know Johnny and I want him to be one of his People, if Whistle wants it too. Don't tell him again he must speak English."

"It'll make him stand out as different when we get to the city." Hannah stood akimbo, her blond hair leaking from its bun, her face stern. "You know he'll be branded as a breed, he goes on babbling like that."

"His father's a breed," I said more strongly than I'd intended. "And Whistle *is* different. But I don't want to fight with you," I offered softly. I picked up a small shirt she'd sewn for Whistle, noting its tiny, loving stitches. "We all want what's best for him."

Mollified, Hannah bent to her packing again, and I left to find my husband. We'd talked for several long nights about Hannah's plan to head east, and agreed she had a good point. But we weren't ready to send our son away to a boarding school, not yet. But looking wouldn't hurt.

I found Johnny giving the axles a thorough greasing. Kissing the back of his head, I leaned against the wagon, waiting for him to tell me in his own time what was on his mind.

"Hannah's packed and ready to roll, I'd bet." He sounded less than amused.

"Almost. As good as." I watched the new shoots of wheat waving in the warm spring sun. I understood Harry's obsession.

"I'm going to ask Harry to go with you. In case there's any trouble."

"Hannah wants him along," I acknowledged. "But not for that reason. What do you expect?"

I trusted his instincts. A former Army scout, he'd lived both as a white man and as a Comanche. If there was trouble, he'd smell it like cowpies on his heels.

"Don't know. Just a worry." As he smiled up at me, I saw more than worry in his eyes.

"Don't fret, I won't be staying. This is to get it out

of Hannah's system. She'd best quit nagging me, after this.''

Johnny laughed like a man who knew more about women than he should. ''Don't bet on it. Just don't stay too long. Be happier, myself, if you came home after Saint Louis.''

I knew the prospect of a long sojourn back East wasn't thrilling him. But we'd been separated by prison, and a few weeks wouldn't undo us. Still and all, I wished he'd come too. But I'd never asked, knowing that the farther Johnny kept from ''civilization,'' the happier he'd be.

I wrapped my arms around him as he stood, pulling him close, feeling the warmth of his skin through his shirt. ''Want me to bring you back anything?''

''You and our son, would do me just fine.'' He kissed my forehead. ''I mean it, don't let Hannah keep you away for longer than you need. I'm thinking, well, maybe it would be for the best, I'll look around, see if there's anywhere we can move, maybe run a few head of cattle, do some small farming, hay and the like.''

I'd never heard my husband mention a permanent home. The Monroes' farm had been our center, the place we would always return to for refuge. Yet I knew what Johnny was saying. We needed a place of our own, even if it were hardscrabble. Even if we had to return to the reservation. I couldn't believe I'd even had that thought.

''Times are changing, Johnny. Maybe we can find something, well, we can afford. We'll talk when I get home.'' I knew Johnny must have been thinking this through for some time. He wouldn't have brought it up unless he was serious about it. The thought of my brother, his redheaded wife, and their gaggle of children came to me again. I spoke without thinking.

"When I get back, let's talk to Noble. Maybe he'd sell us some land."

Johnny's back stiffened under my arms. I knew the rending of their friendship had been bitter, and seemed irrevocable. But that was years the locusts had eaten. He stroked my face with hands callused from the plow, his expression telling me he was far away in his memories.

"Won't take any charity from Noble."

"Didn't say that, did I? I was thinking of Whistle, earlier, and how Noble's children would be company for him. And they are his kin, he should know them."

Pulling out of my arms, Johnny turned and bent to shoulder the wheel he'd already coated to slide back onto the axle. "We don't need your brother," he mumbled so I could barely hear him.

"No, we don't. But maybe Whistle does." Maybe, Noble needed us, I thought. He'd been kindness itself to me, when I'd believed myself widowed and homeless. His prejudice against my husband was more deeply ingrained than his love for me, but time has a way of washing the arrogance out of deeply seated thinking.

"Came to me, we might leave Kansas." With a grunt, Johnny shouldered the wheel into place.

"Oh." I hadn't seen this coming. Somehow, I'd expected the Monroes would always be a part of our lives. But civilization was approaching, along with the twentieth century. Johnny was realist enough to know we'd never survive on the reservation without becoming beggars. He'd never allow that.

"What are we running from?" I asked.

Johnny locked the wheel into place, then stood slowly, wiping his hands on the rag he'd tucked in his belt.

"Nothing." His voice tight, he gave me a light kiss on the cheek. "I'd better get to work, if this thing's going to hold up. Don't want Harry having to change an axle in the middle of nowhere, cursing me for not checking everything ten times."

I grabbed his sleeve. "Tell me," I demanded.

But my husband was one to keep his counsel, when he chose. Shaking his head, he gently moved me to one side, and passed by me.

I wasn't going to let it drop. "Tonight," I warned, "tonight we talk."

His face told me I'd be wasting my words. May as well spit in the wind, I consoled myself as I slowly edged my way back to the house. I could see Harry on the front porch, beating the dirt from his pants with his hat, scratching his head as though he'd just seen fairies jump from the midst of the wheat fields.

"She got you too, huh?"

"Seems so. Bath time tonight, according to my beloved. So I'll be sweet for the trail. Pshaw," Harry said with what amounted to good humor and exasperation.

"I'll be glad for the company." In truth, I would

be happy to have him along. While Hannah and I had planned to ride the train back East after seeing Saint Louis, I was hoping Harry would add his vote to mine, to come home before we boarded. I'd had enough time to think about going back to Virginia, to know it wasn't where I really wanted to be. Separation from Johnny brought back too many painful memories of my false widowhood.

Whistle chose that moment to burrow from under the house.

''Spiders, Mama!'' His child-hand opened to show me his cache.

''Put them back, Whistle. They've a job to do, like everything else. Their webs catch bugs and keep them out of the house.''

He gave me a face-splitting smile, and my heart was in his grubby little palm. No, we'd not be gone long, and Whistle wasn't going to spend time in any boarding school. We'd make this trip to keep Hannah happy, but Johnny was right, we had to live our own lives.

Late that night, after the supper dishes had been washed and our traveling clothes laid out for morning, Johnny and I took our nightly stroll into the dark, just the two of us. We'd found we needed that time to talk of things we couldn't say with Hannah and Harry in the next room. I tried valiantly to leave the opening gambit to Johnny, but he seemed content to hold my hand and stride the land.

''We can make peace with my brother,'' I started gently. ''Even if we stay here, we should. Time's passing, Johnny. Quickly. Who knows how long any of us have left on this earth?''

I didn't know why I was suddenly obsessed with seeing my brother once more, with settling what differences were between us.

Johnny's hand pulled from mine, and I sensed he coiled within like a clock wound too tightly.

''I don't think Noble would have any of it, tell the truth. Been thinking, we could head to California. Maybe farther north. Harry's a good man, and the only man I'd trust to take my wife away from me, but he and Hannah need to work this out. We're in the middle, and it's not good for either of them.''

I knew he was right. I'd sensed the same, since Hannah had come back from her mother's funeral, just as the Ghost Dance was scaring half the farmers in the West.

''I hate to leave her. She's so afraid to be alone.''

''Harry's got to help her, not you. She's his wife, and he loves her as much as I do you.''

I seized his face in the darkness and kissed him. Words like ''love'' don't come easily to a man, and Johnny was no exception.

''I'll talk to them, on the way to Saint Louis. See if I can work out a truce.'' Things had been getting worse between them. I saw Harry staring at Hannah with a hangdog, wilted expression when he didn't notice that I was looking. Hannah had become singularly minded, and a stubborn woman with one thing on her mind was a force to be reckoned with.

''Won't be enough. I'll ask around, while you're

gone, see if there's something we can find to farm. Not as much as Harry has here, but enough for us to live.''

I could hardly believe that my half-Comanche husband had become a farmer, much less one who wanted to own the land. I knew what a sacrifice this was for him. ''We'll live wherever we're together. Nothing can separate us. Not the three of us.''

As he draped his arm around my waist, I leaned my head on his shoulder. ''We've been through too much, to lose ourselves in this fight between Harry and Hannah. You're right, we should get out of their way, let them figure it out.''

Johnny kissed the top of my head. ''I'll do it, while you're gone. Don't stay away long, promise me. I can't bear it.''

I held him tightly, the night stars shining like new pennies in the heavens, and made him my promise.

I hoped I could keep it. I owed Hannah much, and even though I knew my husband was right, I couldn't abandon her to her fears.

I'd faced too many of my own, all alone.

Chapter Five

I tried to keep a smiling face the next morning for the sake of Whistle, who was as eager to be on his way as a tick to jump on a dog. The wagon loaded, the horses' shoes checked one last time, the basket filled with food Hannah had been cooking for days stored under the blanket, and we were ready to roll.

But so much could happen to a man alone on a farm. Fire, lightning, a horse falling in a gopher hole. I worried as much as the day the Army had arrested Johnny. I saw my own fears reflected in his eyes, and bit my tongue. I'd been about to warn him to take care, but he knew that. No need to worry him with my silliness.

"Hurry back," Johnny said and smiled as Harry, spiffed up in a new shirt made by Hannah, accepted the leads. "Wheat won't grow without you."

Harry looked as miserable as a man putting on wool

underwear in July. "Get back as fast as I, uh, we can."
He accepted the leathers with an imperceptible shake
of his head, as though acknowledging Johnny's
sympathy.

Whistle stood in the back of the wagon between my
legs, hanging on to the sides to lean over for a farewell
kiss from his father.

"Be a good boy, do as your mother tells you,"
Johnny admonished in English. "And watch for signs,
as I taught you," he added in Comanche.

I knew I'd have to keep an eye on my son, who
would be searching for animal prints at every stop of
the wagon.

"Thanks for the warning," I said with a laugh,
squeezing my husband's hand. We'd said our good-
byes the night before. He worried for me, as much as
I for him, I knew. The terrors of the big city were
immense in his mind.

"I'll write when we get to Saint Louis," I promised
again, as much as for him for myself. I'd taught him
to read English during the long winter nights when
there was no farm work he could do.

Hannah pressed Harry's arm, and Harry knew she
meant for him to crack the leathers on the horses'
flanks. With a lurch, we were off. Whistle could hardly
believe his good luck, and waved and bounced in the
back of the wagon until his father's figure had become
a speck. Then the reality of saying good-bye hit him
like a hammer, and he turned to me with shining eyes.

"I want to go home to Papa," he whispered in my
ear. "Can I jump down and run back?"

"No, sweetheart, you have to stay with me. Papa will want to hear all about the signs you found, and the animals you see. He'll be there, when we get back, don't worry."

Whistle sat on my lap, his small face a study of concentration as he absorbed the enormity of leaving his father behind, and the excitement of the unknown. I wrapped my arms around him tightly, feeling his little heart thudding in his chest. I would walk through a wall of fire for this child, as would Johnny. The farm disappeared from view, the sun grew hot. Though I stared at the land, my mind was not on its way to Saint Louis with the rest of my body. I hoped I was making the right decision, when I tapped Harry on the back.

He half turned, to look at me better. "Need to stop?"

"No, I want to go to Larned. Saint Louis can wait."

"What?" Hannah swiveled to give me one of her better stares. "Have you taken leave of your senses? It's out of the way!"

"It's where my brother lives. I want to talk to him, and I don't want Johnny to know it." I'd never before practiced duplicity on my husband, and I hoped he'd forgive me. If my plans worked out, he surely would.

"But we're going to look at school for Whistle!" Hannah wasn't going to give up without a fight.

"Hannah, this is important. You know I wouldn't ask this, if it weren't."

She knew me well, that much was for sure.

"You haven't heard from him in years," she muttered under her breath, but loudly enough that I could hear.

"If she wants to see her brother, we're going to Larned." Harry's words were clearly the last to be spoken on the subject.

I settled back in the wagon bed, Whistle happily playing with a bag filled with stones he'd collected, and thought of Noble, the brother I'd lost for so long. He and Johnny had scouted for the Army together, long before there'd been Rebecca of the red hair, long before there was a treaty at Medicine Lodge with the Kiowa. When I'd been captured by the Kiowa, Johnny and Noble had taken off to find me. Johnny had succeeded first. But my year with the Kiowa had changed me, and I was no longer the girl I'd been before the Kiowa stripped me of my false pride, my white arrogance. Johnny and I found something together we'd never have allowed as a possibility when he tracked me among the Kiowa. Noble had never forgiven Johnny for taking me as his wife.

But Noble and I were blood kin, and I'd been a fool to let the years drift away between us. If I knew anything at all about Rebecca, Noble's wife, I knew she'd been mending fences between us from the moment Johnny and I had disappeared from their farm. The time had ripened like a peach about to fall from the tree, and I was going to take the first step to reach and pluck it down. If nothing else came of this, at least I'd find out how irreparably damaged our relationship had been by my refusal to deny my husband when he reappeared from the dead.

My bottom resented the buckboard, and soon I was tugging on Harry to slow down so Whistle and I could walk. I'd become accustomed to long distances on foot when Johnny and I roamed the land he hadn't seen since prison. My feet itched to be on the ground, despite Hannah's protestations that my petticoats would be a mess.

We stopped early to eat our picnic, the pie still warm from the oven. Despite my worry over leaving Johnny, I was happy to be moving down the road. My Army upbringing and my years with the tribe had accustomed me to travel as a way of life. We ate heartily, the sky was a soft blue, the horses grazed contentedly, and I was feeling calmer than I had since Hannah had hatched this plan. Stomachs full, Hannah and I folded the blanket. Harry and Whistle wandered off to do their male business, while Hannah and I repacked the leftovers to load back into the wagon.

The sound of a horse running flat out startled us. Checking our calm duo, I couldn't seem to grasp that the noise came from another animal, lathered and laboring, until I saw the bay. Flat out, its rider quirting for all he was worth, the horse was clearly on its last legs. Despite the years of peace on the Monroe farm, I still knew danger when I saw it.

"Hannah, get over here," I snapped, jerking her to the small stand of cottonwoods where we'd sheltered.

"What on earth?" Hannah stared at me as if I'd lost my mind, then saw the horse and rider over my shoulder. "He can get by the wagon," she started to say, when I forcibly hauled her into the stand of trees where Harry and Whistle were unaware of what was riding down on us.

I'd seen horses in better shape after the Apache got finished with them. "Get down," I hissed, gesturing to Harry and Whistle as I pressed my hand to Hannah's shoulder to force her to her knees. Fortunately, we'd worn our everyday garb for traveling, and none of the fabrics were any too bright after many washings with lye soap.

Crouching in the stand of bushes and weeds, we watched as the rider flung himself from the stumbling horse and jerked a knife from his belt. Without a look around, he slit the leathers on Brownie and pulled him out of the traces. Harry's face purpled, and he started to shout out something, when I clamped my hand over his mouth.

"Quiet!" Harry's rifle was in the wagon, and I had no intention of getting Whistle caught in any crossfire, anyway.

The man tore his saddle from the heaving sides of his mount and threw it on our Brownie. Jerking the bit from the bleeding mouth of his bay, he forced it onto the reluctant wagon horse, who was thoroughly confused at the turn his day had taken. Studying the man's dusty, trail-worn clothes, I couldn't place him. We weren't so far from home that we wouldn't recognize any neighboring traveler on the way to Larned. His face, hidden as he bent to cinch the saddle and mount, meant nothing to me in the quick glimpse I had of him before he raked his spurs into Brownie.

Brownie squealed at this rough treatment, and

Whistle cried out. ''Hush!'' I commanded in Kiowa. Whistle had been trained early on to keep his mouth shut and his tears stifled when danger lurked nearby.

Harry wasn't as easy to control as Whistle. As Brownie bucked at rough treatment he'd never before received, Harry rushed for the wagon before Hannah or I could grab him.

''Stop it!'' Harry bellowed, clawing for the man's leg as Brownie squealed in fright. Twisting in the saddle, the horse thief slapped uselessly at Harry, even as he continued to beat at Brownie. What the idiot didn't know was that the harder you tried to make Brownie go, the more stubborn he'd get, until he'd roll on his side and get rid of you. We'd all long ago learned that a loose rein and an easy seat got the most out of our recalcitrant Brownie.

''Keep Whistle here,'' I hissed at Hannah. Harry's mouth was bleeding where a spur had caught him, and the thief was scrambling for the pistol holstered on his side.

Eyes as big as the moon, Hannah started after me, but halted when I threw her a look that told her to stay with my son if she wanted to live. The melee around Brownie took no notice of me as I slipped around the far side of the wagon and scratched under the seat for Harry's shotgun. I knew it was loaded. Shouldering it, I aimed a hair higher than the thief's head. Brownie, tired of the caterwauling and the pain, was beginning to buckle at the knees, a sure sign he was going down. If Harry was smart, he'd jump out of the way and let Brownie do the job for him.

But Harry had a grip like a terrier on a rat, and he wasn't about to let go. Brownie crashed to his side like he'd been shot as Harry tried to jump out of the way. The rider wasn't as lucky, as his left leg, still in the stirrup, crunched between the ground and Brownie's side. I heard the bones crack. On his side, Harry pushed at Brownie's rump like a man trying to tread water. More fat cushioned his leg, but if Brownie tried to do his famous back roll, both of them were as dead as fleas caught between my thumbs.

I squeezed the trigger, the blast startling both Brownie and the two men. "Hold up!" I screamed. "Drop your weapon, now!"

Harry stared at me as if seeing me for the first time. "Not you, Harry! Hannah," I shouted, "grab Brownie's reins."

As though the pain had just run from the nerves in his foot to his brain, the thief began to curse.

"Hurry, Hannah!" I had my finger on the other trigger, ready to let both Brownie and the thief have the barrel if he reached for his gun. "Throw it here, mister, and I'll get the horse off you."

My words must have finally sunk in. Harry'd wiggled free and sat splayed about a yard away from the horse, massaging his calf. A quick glance, and I saw he was twisting his foot from side to side. But the thief hadn't fared as well. Hannah reached for Brownie's reins as though she were picking up a dead possum, and held them as far from her as she could get.

"Get Brownie up, Hannah," I nudged her gently. "I won't shoot you."

Her look told me she was skeptical of that promise, but she began to cluck to Brownie and flick the reins. "Up, Brownie," she crooned.

"Get him off me!" the thief screamed as Brownie shifted his weight, preparing to roll back to his feet.

I didn't much care how badly Brownie maimed him in getting up, but I surely didn't want to have to listen to the man scream for the next ten miles, or until we found someplace to turn him over to the law.

"Hold still," I commanded, sidling over to Harry and passing him the shotgun. "Make it count, if he tries anything."

Harry glared at the man moaning as Brownie tried to get his feet under him. "Stay out of the way, Myth-maker, 'cause I'll shoot."

"Good." I stood with Hannah at Brownie's head and clicked encouragingly, in the way all horses understand. Hannah caught my drift and added her soothing voice. Soon Brownie decided to ignore the lump on his saddle, and with one huge effort, staggered to his feet. I jumped for the thief, snatching his shoulder in a grip I'd not soon release, hauling him over the side and onto his face in the dust. Before he could grab my ankle and pull me to him as a hostage, I hopped away.

"Got him," Harry assured me as he limped to my side, shotgun business-end down at the back of the man's head. "Now just who in Sam Hill are you, and why are you stealing my horse?"

I didn't much care for explanations, I already had a good idea he was running from the law. "My guess is, the posse's not far behind.'' Turning, I stared behind us. "Been running like a rabbit, must be close to catching you. What you done?''

The thief rolled to his back, his mouth snarled in pain. "Nothin','' he spit at me. "Not a blamed thing.''

"And I'm your ancient aunt,'' I snorted.

"Leave him,'' Hannah pleaded, leading Brownie to the side. "Can't harness Brownie, he cut the leathers. Have to make Larned with us walking, can't put all our weight on one horse.''

The thief's mount, winded and on his last legs, leaned against the side of the wagon. "And that one's not good for much, won't be for a month of Sundays.'' Harry shook his head. A man who treasured his own farm stock, he didn't hold with abusing animals. I would have shot the horse to put him out of his misery.

"Whistle? Come here.'' I spoke in Kiowa.

"Mama?'' Whistle edged out from behind a cottonwood.

"Sweetheart, come here. Everything's all right.'' I moved away from the mess on the ground before me to reassure my son. But Whistle wasn't to be deterred. Leaning around my skirts, he got an eyeful of the thief.

"Mama, that man's not right. His skin's too dark.'' Whistle spoke in English.

For the first time, I saw the thief's face, and not his mangled foot. Whistle had never seen a black man before. His clothes said cowboy, but I couldn't help wondering what he was doing in Kansas. Maybe he'd been with the Buffalo soldiers, mustered out, and stayed.

"I know you?" Harry frowned, the shotgun still aimed where it would do serious damage.

The thief muttered, "Ain't never been this far out of Indian Territory."

"Who's after you? Speak up, man." Harry was curt.

The thief's face was grim, and it had nothing to do with his injury. Silence was all Harry would get out of him.

I knew Hannah would have to hear the whole story sooner or later, and that she'd hold her fears in abeyance until then. "No sense goin' into it here," I said and sighed. "What do you think, Harry, can we lift him into the wagon?"

Harry still looked as though he'd just as soon shoot the thief. "Horse thievin's a hangin' offense. Far as I'm concerned, he can rot right here."

"Well, I'm not wasting any good rope on him, and I don't see how we can leave him out here to die, not as good Christian folk." Hannah gave Harry one of her looks that ordered him to fall into line like a good soldier. I had to admire her logic, thrift with Christian forgiveness. I wanted the law to handle him.

"You ride with Whistle. Mythmaker and I'll take turns walking, keeping the shotgun on him." Harry decided it was easier to give Hannah her way in this. He was a wise man, mostly. "But the first jail we find, he goes in it."

"If he lives that long." I was staring at his foot. If we took his boot off, that ankle would probably come off with it. "Best leave him like he is, until we can stop awhile and get it splinted."

Swearing like a Cavalry trooper, the thief was loaded into the buckboard. Harry and I tried to be gentle, but the foot was his own fault, I figured, and he deserved whatever pain he'd garnered as wages for his sins. A healer by nature and long practice, I hated to see anyone, man or beast, hurting, but this savage man had frightened the tar out of us.

"Maybe we should head back for the farm, send for the law." Harry and I walked behind the wagon and tried to ignore the man's groans. Harry sounded uncertain.

"You know Hannah'll do that when the world comes to an end. You want to convince her to quit this trip, you be my guest."

I was fine with the walking, but I could tell Harry was feeling it in the leg that Brownie had pinched. Pulling up, he massaged his calf muscle. Harry, wise man that he was, shook his head and answered me softly. "You're right. Maybe we can drop him in Larned."

"If we get him there. Way he was riding, I thought for sure the posse'd be here by now." I glanced over my shoulder, half expecting a cloud of dust announcing the arrival of the law.

"If they catch up, I don't want Whistle to see him hanged." Harry's lined face was grim.

"Me either." I'd seen enough death and destruction to last me a lifetime. "What do you want to do?"

"Think getting him to Larned's the best bet. He'll

be out of our hair, and we won't have to see what they do to him.'' Harry's eyes were on Hannah, and I knew he was trying to spare her as much as Whistle.

"Not much we can do, the posse finds his horse, they'll find us." Brownie plodded along behind the wagon, docile and calm now that he wasn't being spurred. "Guess we could send him on his way, on Brownie."

"No!" Harry's eyes said he'd never turn over one of his animals to a brute who used force. "He's wanted by the law, the law'll have him. I'll keep the posse from stringin' him up."

"How? With a shotgun? They'll think we're in on whatever he did." I thought for a bit, then jumped on the back of the wagon, clambering in before I lost my nerve.

Unfolding the picnic blanket, I spread it over our malevolent guest. "If you have any wits at all about you, you'll keep your mouth shut should we meet any riders. My friends and I have no wish to watch you swing at the end of a rope, but have no fear, we'll turn you in to the law. Pick your poison."

"I'll keep my peace," he said with a snarl, glaring at me as though I were the one responsible for his troubles. "I committed no crime, I swear to you, lady."

"That's not for me to decide. But I've seen the Army serve as judge, jury, and executioner, and I have no wish to see you die without a fair trial. We'll get you to the sheriff at Larned, and you can try to convince a jury there of your innocence."

Grasping the edge of the blanket so he could pull it over his face upon a moment's notice, the thief swallowed hard. ''Name's Gravitt. They say I done killed a widow woman in the Territory, white woman I never laid eyes on in my life. I swear to you on my mother's grave, I am innocent of this murder.''

I harrumphed loudly.

''Keep yourself still if I stop the wagon,'' Hannah added unnecessarily as she glanced over her shoulder at me. We understood each other so well, I knew she thought as I about our unwanted guest.

''If you don't, I'll shoot you myself,'' Harry added menacingly. ''Won't have your kind draggin' my family into your mess.''

I prayed we'd get to Larned before the posse—or Harry—took matters into its own hands.

Chapter Six

Rebecca bathed the weakened Peck as she would one of her children, all business and cleanliness-is-next-to-godliness. She'd sent the Indian child, Feather, to the creek with the older boys, and orders that lye soap was to be used all over, especially behind the ears. She wanted to see for herself, without any prying eyes, how badly Hunter Peck was suffering.

Peck had enough fight in him to give her a hard time, she noted gratefully. But in the end, she won the battle, and saw no signs of plague, just malnutrition and a bad cough. Sending Noble to the chicken coop with orders to wring the neck of a scrawny one, she set about cooking up a pot of chicken broth filled with vegetables fresh from her garden. There wasn't much she couldn't tame with good common sense and chicken soup.

She figured Peck's lungs had been lying down too

long, and he'd coughed enough to turn his throat inside out. So she had the boys prop up some boards in
the sunshine, where she ensconced Mr. Peck, cleaned
and quilted, to soak up the pretty day. He seemed to
have calmed down when she told him the other children were caring for the child he called Feather.

Sitting beside him, spooning in her broth, she
broached the subject she'd been storing for a moment
when he felt better. A few days in the sun, and she
could see him mending quickly.

"Tell me about this Mythmaker, the woman you
want Feather to live with." She held the spoon in
abeyance, waiting for his answer. She'd never forgotten her sister-in-law, though Noble never spoke of her.

Peck pulled at his long, curly hair, squinting at her
from the sides of his eyes. "Met her in the Territory,
that Ghost Dance thing them Kiowa had going, afore
Wounded Knee Massacre. She and her man, they'd
come from Kansas, a farm they was sharing with some
white folks, to see what was goin' on. Me, I'd hitched
up with this preacher man, name of Donaldson, only
once he gets to the Kiowa, he's called Magpie. Turns
out this Mythmaker woman had adopted him, way
back when he was a kid. He did okay in the white
man's world. Figgered she'd do the same for that little
fella I got."

"Do you know the name of the people Mythmaker
and her husband farmed with? Here, in Kansas?"
Rebecca tried to keep the excitement from her voice.

"Nope. Didn't get too friendly, me and Mythmaker.

But she's a woman who'll do right by a body. I got me a responsibility for that boy.''

''And where'd he come from, your Feather?'' Rebecca was remembering the carrot-haired man who'd gone with Noble to see if his wife's head was in a pickle jar heading for Washington, D.C. But the child, at this moment, was as much her duty as Peck's health.

''Wounded Knee. Got him out, when the lead was flyin' like snowflakes. Ain't got no kin left, 'cept me. I ain't blood, but I'll do him right.'' Peck splayed his hands on the quilt, studying his lost fingers. ''Can't do no shootin' with my left hand now.''

Rebecca harumphed. ''Times are changing, Mr. Peck. A man with a gun carries a liability with him. You'll be better off.''

Peck stared at her as though she'd lost her mind. ''Beggin' your pardon, Mrs. McFarland, and you being so good to me and all, but times ain't never gonna change that much. Man without a gun may as well start carving his own tombstone.''

Suspicion began to creep into Rebecca like poison ivy under a wall. ''You running from something, Mr. Peck?''

Peck considered her face, her freckles bright in the sunlight, a few gray hairs showing in the auburn. ''Could be, missus, could be. Don't rightly know how it done turned out.''

''Tell me about it.'' She didn't ask, she commanded. Like her boys, Peck felt compelled to tell the truth.

''Woman I lodged with, in a manner of speakin',

showed up dead one night. I ain't done it, I swear, Mrs. McFarland, but it sure didn't look good. Me, I ain't done steady work in the Territory, you get my drift, and I sure liked the Widow Eileen. We got on real good.'' He almost looked wistful. ''But me being a breed, and half black at that, it wouldn'a done the widow a bit of good if anyone'd known about us. So we kept it quiet, and liked it like that.''

''So when she was murdered, you thought you'd be blamed, and ran.'' Rebecca frowned.

''That about says it all. Ended up with them Kiowa, 'cause of that preacher man. He was with me at the widow's, when she was killed.''

''You should have stayed and proven your innocence.'' Rebecca pursed her lips as she offered him another spoonful.

''You wasn't there, pardon me saying so, Mrs. McFarland.''

''No, I wasn't,'' she conceded. ''Perhaps this minister will be able to testify to your innocence, however.''

Peck snorted. ''He's Kiowa. May dress up like a white man, talk like a white man, but he's still just some red-skinned Indian. 'Sides, we had us a little ruckus at a bar that day, and he ended up with some busted bones. Who's gonna believe a preacher with a left hook?''

''I see your problem.'' Rebecca sat staring at the weathered clapboards behind Peck's head. ''You must do what you think is right, of course. But if you want to raise that little boy, and I see no reason you can't, you won't be able to spend your life running from the law.'' When Noble had first come to her, memory gone thanks to some buffalo hiders who'd beaten him to within an inch of his life, she'd wondered if he was a wanted man.

''That boy needs more than I can give him. He needs a woman's touch. You got quite a brood here, Mrs. McFarland, one more or less won't make much difference, will it?''

She fixed him with her firmest ''mother'' stare. ''Children aren't given to us to parcel out like dividing a herd of beeves, Mr. Peck. That boy is your responsibility. Now you make sure you get well, and straighten your life out, for his sake.''

Plunking the soup bowl on the bench, Rebecca hopped up and marched back to her house. She'd given Peck plenty to think about, and she wanted him to ruminate some. She trusted her children to the job of teaching the Indian child English, and she'd make sure he was decently clothed and fed, but what she'd do with him if Peck lit out was another matter altogether. She'd never turned away anyone needing help, not in her entire life, but that child needed Peck. The boy's attachment to the black man was obvious, the adoration there for anyone with half a mind to notice. Running out on a child could destroy Magpie's ability to trust for the rest of his life, and she didn't know how to heal the soul.

Sighing, she sought her husband in the barn. Hunter Peck had brought a huge helping of trouble into her ordered life, but if anyone could unknot the tangled skein, she could. Noble worked a hammer on a bent stall hinge.

"The boys still have Magpie at the creek?" She fingered a halter hanging by the barn door.

Glancing up, Noble admired his wife, framed by sunlight in the barn door, dust motes flying around her like a million golden sparkles. Her dark red hair was lightening as she aged, and she looked almost angelic to him at that moment. "Last I heard, they were all naked as blue jays, and whooping it up. The child'll be fine with them." Noble eased off the hinge he was repairing.

Rebecca moved to stand beside him. The warmth they shared was more than physical. Just now, she was as tense as a harness about to snap. "Look like I feel, Rebecca. Horseshoe caught you in the gut?"

She hadn't known how she was going to broach the topic of his sister before he spoke. "Was just talking to Peck. Says Beth's in Kansas, leastwise, she was. A farm, with some white folks." The knot in her stomach eased a bit as Noble looked sad, then calm. She'd feared an outburst, though he wasn't given to such displays.

"You think I should find her?" His words sought not so much advice as confirmation for what he'd been thinking for the past few days since Peck had mentioned the name Mythmaker.

"I think it's time we were a family again. All of us. Our Beth is a married woman now, don't you think we've pretended your sister never existed long enough?" She knew he felt Elizabeth had betrayed him by leaving with her half-Indian husband. She just wasn't sure if his love for his sister would win over his pride.

"It'd take awhile to find her. I can't be gone that long."

"You can take as long as you need. The boys are old enough to shoulder this farm. I did it before you came along."

"That isn't what I expected to hear, wife." Noble pocketed the hinge and moved to pull her close to him. "I want you to say you can't live without me."

"You know very well I can. But it won't be half as much fun." She nuzzled his shoulder.

He was silent, and she could feel his thoughts beating with his heart. "There's another problem. He ran into her in Indian Territory. For all we know, she could still be there."

Releasing her, Noble paced the barn with the short, determined steps she knew meant he was thinking hard. He pretended to check a board here and there, inspect the neat leathers lining the walls, but she knew his mind was already on the trail.

"I can wire the reservation, find out if she's there. Someone will have noticed a white woman living with one of . . . them." Stopping, he looked at her, but she knew he was seeing something, someone, else. Was it the past, she wondered, or the future?

"That man, the one you helped. He'd been looking for his wife, the one captured by the Comanches. Wasn't he from Kansas? You know, his wife was the one you brought home with Elizabeth, back when Johnny was arrested.''

''Monroe. Harry Monroe. I remember.'' How could he forget the heads pickled in brine, both he and Monroe searching the mottled features for loved ones. They'd both been lucky that neither Hannah nor Elizabeth was among those decapitated for identification. The Texas Rangers had tracked some renegade Comanches running from the reservation, and after killing them, discovered two were whites. One of them had been a woman with pale hair. Elizabeth and Hannah had blond hair. The pickled heads had been sent around for identification, in hopes that some white family, somewhere, would be able to identify the white Comanche.

''Could Elizabeth and Johnny be with her? With her and her husband, I mean?'' Rebecca remembered Elizabeth's indifference to the other woman, although it was clear they'd once been close. She'd never asked Elizabeth the cause of the rift between them, assuming her sister-in-law would have told her if she'd felt the need.

Noble rubbed his face, his eyes seeing only the past. ''She was in Salinas, as I remember.''

''I don't know why, but I feel as though Hannah and Elizabeth were connected in a way that went deeper than we saw. Women who've walked through fire together don't walk away when there's a need. Maybe Elizabeth and Johnny gave up on the reservation and went to find her friend.'' She meant no criticism, but the plain truth was, as long as Elizabeth was with her half-breed husband, Noble wouldn't have welcomed them. "It's a starting place, at least."

Rebecca had watched her husband age ten years when his sister had walked out, leaving behind all her dresses, all the trappings that made her a white woman in the eyes of the world. If seeing Elizabeth again could remove those anxiety lines that creased his forehead, she'd be more than grateful. The time had come to forgive and forget, and welcome Elizabeth and Johnny Two Hats with opened arms. But her husband was a stubborn man, and she'd learned when to push, and when to stand back.

"I'll think on it. Won't hurt to send a telegram or two. See what happens." He pulled the hinge out and thumbed it. The iron was still waffled from where it'd taken a wallop from their bull. "I feel like this. Strong as metal, but bent out of my purpose by something I can't rightly do anything about." He stared at Rebecca. "Am I wrong?"

"No," she whispered softly. "Not wrong. Just takes some careful tapping, you'll be straightened out in no time."

"Want to try?"

She laughed. "Been doing that since the day you dragged into my place, half dead and nearly frozen to death. Don't think I'll give up on you, Noble McFarland, not by a long shot."

He arched her waist with his arm, pulling her to him. "Don't even think of it, girl."

She laughed, sounding like the young widow he'd loved so many years ago. Walking with him into the sunshine, she squinted, her eyes focusing on the man wrapped in her quilt, propped in the sun.

''Whatever you're going to do, do it soon. That man's in trouble with the law, and I need to know if Magpie's going to need to learn to love us as family, or if he should go to Mythmaker. Doesn't do a child good to love, then have to give it up, and move on, and love again.''

Noble frowned. ''How bad is it, the law trouble?''

''Sounds bad enough to me. Says he's wanted for murdering a woman he boarded with, in the Territory.''

Noble started. ''Won't have a killer in my house. Send him packin' right now.''

Rebecca laid a restraining hand on his arm. ''Says he's innocent. I believe him. Didn't have to tell me about it. Only a man who's not afraid of the truth would do that.''

Easing off, Noble stared at Peck, asleep in the sun. ''He's a dead man, if he harms any of you.''

''He saved that child's life, Noble. Got him out of harm's way at Wounded Knee. I hardly believe he's a cold-blooded killer.''

Noble turned to watch his sons as they rolled back from the creek like a pack of playful puppies, the Indian child frolicking in their midst.

''Think I'll head for Larned. Send those wires.''

Rebecca nodded, wondering if the impetus came from a curiosity as to his sister's whereabouts, or concern for an orphaned child who might lose his only parental figure to a hangman's noose. Either way, she didn't care what sent him to Larned. She just prayed they'd receive an answer that would assure them that Elizabeth was alive and well.

She wandered closer to Peck, intending to check on his temperature with a hand to his forehead. He was stronger, but not out of the woods yet. Her light touch awakened him.

"Good sleep?" She meant to move on about her business.

Peck watched Noble saddle up. "Good enough, I managed to wake up. Not dead yet." His laugh carried a harshness she didn't like. "Where's he goin'?"

She followed his eyes to Noble, swinging into the saddle. "Larned. Send some wires, see if Mythmaker can be found."

"Send one for me." Peck's voice carried over the hubbub of the children.

"Who you want to wire?" Noble walked the horse to Peck's pallet and stared down. "Any kin need to know your whereabouts?"

"Nope. But I'd take it kindly, if you'd let a preacher down near Fort Sill, name of Peter Donaldson, know where I am and that I can't ride just yet."

Noble thought a minute. "What church?"

"Episcopal, as I 'member it. Mission down near the fort."

"All right, Mr. Peck. I'll do it. You can tell me later why."

Peck nodded, wondering the "why" of it himself.

Rebecca watched Noble ride out for Larned, pushing to a canter before he hit the edge of the yard. Three wires, three answers, she hoped.

Chapter Seven

Morning came and Johnny hadn't slept much. Without his wife's presence, he listened to the night sounds and sat on the front porch beginning with false dawn. His chores were mostly done before the sun came up, and the chickens wondered why on earth they'd been awakened before the rooster's crow.

Without her and Whistle, the farm felt foreign to him. Harry had taught him all he could about farming, but Johnny believed some men were born to the soil and some weren't. But because the Monroes and they were family, he did what had to be done and kept his complaints to himself.

Not that they were many, the complaints, that is. His long years in the federal prison at Fort Leavenworth had been sheer misery. Anything, even starvation on the reservation, had been an improvement over a world without freedom. At least he could plow fields and look into the blue sky, hold his wife and son, hear a hawk's cry as it hunted. Life, he'd learned in prison, was small chances at happiness, and he savored each one like the tastiest morsel.

At first, he'd sought reasons for what had happened to him, to his people, the Comanche. Why had they who formed the world allowed such injustice, such cruelty on a people, on him? He'd truly believed Buffalo Bull Returns could bring back the way of life he'd known when he returned to the Comanche. The prophet's failure had jerked him up like a tight rein. But when Wovoka promised that the Great Spirit would restore the world as it had been before the white people came, he'd done no more than hope. Yet once more, his prayers had failed and the Ghost Dance had brought death to the tribes in the North.

Johnny ate some of the provisions Hannah had prepared for him, stored away in the pie safe. This nonsense about a white school for his son was harmless at this stage, for Whistle was too young for boarding school. Yet when the boy grew older, he knew it would become a serious bone of contention between them. Hannah loved the boy like her own and wanted Whistle to be white. Harry, Johnny was sure, would have done his best to teach Whistle what he could about his Comanche grandmother, if anything had happened to Mythmaker and him during the Ghost Dance. But Hannah would have won in the end. Whistle would have grown up as John Noble McFarland, not John Noble McFarland Two Hats, if Hannah had her way.

As he busied himself cleaning out the barn loft, Johnny knew today was the day. Today, he'd find the rancher he'd heard had brood stock for sale. If he could get them in foal for next spring, even better. Then he'd need a stud, and grazing land. He was Comanche. Horses were in his blood, as crops were in Harry's. Harry would understand, even if the womenfolk didn't.

Mythmaker would follow him, no matter where he went. She too sensed that Hannah's hold on Whistle was growing overly strong. If Harry had managed to give her a child, Hannah's determination to steer Whistle's course in life wouldn't have been so determined. But after all these years, it seemed that Whistle would never have a blood brother by the Monroes. Johnny regretted that he and Harry wouldn't have sons who could grow to manhood together.

Harry had been more than fair with him, splitting all profits from the crops. There hadn't been much grain to sell, not when they'd had to spend more of their time clearing overgrown land than in planting it. But now the farm was producing well, and Johnny felt he'd repaid some of his debt to Harry.

The sun finally up, Johnny made himself a pot of coffee and drank it scalding. Retrieving his buckskin bags from the room he shared with his wife, he carefully folded a clean kerchief, a shirt, and the bag with the coins he'd saved. For a second, he considered cutting his hair and pretending he was Spanish. But his light-colored eyes gave away his real breeding. Besides, he was tired of hiding who he was. Mythmaker never concealed her family connection to the Kiowa, why should he pretend he wasn't one of the People?

The animals had extra buckets of water and feed. Finally assured the farm could survive without him for the next couple of days, he saddled up. The man he'd heard about lived on the border. Selling out cheap to head back East, the farrier had told him when he'd come to shoe the plow horses.

Feeling strangely guilty at leaving the farm, Johnny pushed his gelding. This is for the best, he kept telling himself as the gray's big stride cut down the miles like a scythe. When they got back from the East, he'd have it all set up, and there wouldn't be anything to be done about it.

With each mile he put between himself and the farm, he felt more like a man with a purpose in life. How he wished he'd had Noble along for this buying trip! As youths, the two of them had stolen rides on the best ponies on the Army post, racing through the moonlight. Longwalker, who'd belonged to Noble's father, had been the one steed they hadn't dared touch. Ah, the power of putting a saddle on good horseflesh, the sheer joy of teaching a colt to respond to knee pressure, to a shift of balance. Noble wondered if his hands had forgotten how to train a young horse, or if they'd been callused by the plow for too long. Now he'd find out. If this rancher wanted too dear a price, he'd find horses somewhere else, if he had to go to Mexico.

Late at night when he couldn't sleep, he wondered

at how easily Noble had relinquished his roaming days. The farmer that he'd met when he'd retrieved his wife bore no resemblance, except for physical features, to the young man who'd sworn he'd die an Army scout. Seeing the redheaded woman who was Noble's wife, Johnny had had a suspicion he knew what had happened. Women had a way of changing a man, whether they knew it or not. Sometimes, the change was for the better, sometimes not.

Johnny would have changed the world for his wife. She hadn't asked much of him, only that they live where Whistle was safe and food wasn't a struggle. With his new herd, and the land he'd lease or buy for them, he'd keep his promise to her. He hadn't given up hope for more children, children he'd teach to gentle a horse, to ride like the wind, to ride like the Comanche had ridden for centuries.

Sleeping that night under the stars, Johnny thought of his mother, and the life she'd lived because she'd fallen in love with an Army trooper. He'd never ask his wife to surrender all she held dear for him. She might do it, but he'd never ask.

As he finally fell into a dark and lonely sleep, Johnny dreamed of racing through prairie grass waist-high, his horse's neck barely flecked with sweat, the steady gallop a rhythm that matched the drumbeats of his tribesmen who cheered him on. The sun on his bare back, the whistle of the wind in his ears, were a gift he'd cherish forever.

Waking with the first streaks of dawn, he rolled to his side, hugging himself. He hadn't dreamed of his people in many years, not the way they once were. Since seeing Quanah Parker, he'd been unable to shake off the picture of his people wearing white clothing and cooking on iron stoves. But the dream had given him back a part of himself he'd thought lost forever. Now he knew with unshakable certainty he had to buy those horses.

Following the directions given by the farrier, he found the small ranch without wasting time. The desire for horseflesh burned too brightly in his eyes, and he forced himself to wait an extra day before he approached the rancher. From his vantage point on a small hill, he'd watched the herd in the corral. Concealing himself well, he'd studied how they moved and swirled, their pivots and bucks, and had been satisfied they were a healthy lot.

The morning he decided he was ready to stare at their teeth, he tied his long hair at the back of his neck and pulled his hat down low. Nothing about him would scare the rancher at a distance, and once he was within earshot, all would be well.

At least, he hoped so. He'd grown accustomed, as a child, to the slingshots of prejudice because of the way he looked. But riding the big gray, dressed like a Kansas farmer, he was hoping he'd find nothing more than a man who wanted to strike a bargain.

The rancher was in the barn, mucking straw. Framed by the door, Johnny waited for an invitation.

"Came about the horses." Johnny spoke firmly. "Heard from the farrier at my farm, you had a herd to sell."

The rancher, a young man with a strangely pale face, put down the pitchfork.

"Didn't hear you ride up. What's your name, mister?"

Johnny hesitated only slightly. "Two Hats. Johnny Two Hats." He wished he could give his Comanche name, but it had been buried with the buffalo.

The white man studied Johnny, then slowly leaned the pitchfork against a wall. "Henry Whiting. Come on in to the house, we can talk."

Leading the gray to the hitching rail, Johnny breathed in the warm smell of horses. "No need. Like to see the horses, you don't mind."

Henry Whiting squinted at him from the dark stall he'd been cleaning, then brushed his hands on his Levi's. "Come on, then. Got 'em in the corral."

Johnny sensed the man wanted to ask questions, but he ignored him. Stroking under the halter of the horse closest to him, he pulled the animal over to the fence. "Hold her," he commanded Whiting as he lifted each hoof, ran a hand over the fetlocks, fingered pasterns. Mouth and eyes were inspected, his hand spanned the space between the front legs. Slowly, carefully, he worked his fingers over every mare.

"All of 'em in this good shape?" The herd was more than he'd dared hope for.

Whiting nodded. "Brought some with me, when we moved out here five years ago. Bought a stud, bred the best. Then my wife and child died." His voice was hollow.

Johnny didn't know what to say. "You going back East?"

Whiting shook his head. "Don't rightly know. Anywhere but this place will do. Bad luck runs with this herd. Or maybe it's the land. Don't know, don't rightly care. But I'm gettin' out afore I go crazy alone out here. No one comes out here, not since Martha passed—"

"The stud?" Johnny knew he'd have died long ago, without his wife and child.

"Shot him. Kicked my boy in the head."

Again Johnny didn't know what to say. Discussing money seemed like the last thing he should do. Mythmaker would have sensed words to ease Whiting's grief, but he had none to give. Some pain was like a scar, to be worn for the rest of a life.

"Plan on starting a spread of my own. You got a buyer for this place?"

Whiting looked tired. "Nope. Word gets out. Things start going wrong, they go wrong by the bucketful. You're the first man who's been out here to look at the herd."

Johnny squared his shoulders. The land looked good to him, plenty of water for the horses. "Take you up on your offer, go inside and talk."

Whiting's eyes lost their defeated glaze for a second. "Don't think an Injun's ever been inside my door, not yet, anyway."

"Always a first time, Mr. Whiting." Johnny waited, remembering the guardhouse at Fort Sill, the prison at Fort Leavenworth. He hadn't done too well inside the white man's world, himself. But bad luck didn't scare him. Nothing scared him after Leavenworth, and finding that Mythmaker was alive and waiting for him had made him fearless.

"My money's as good as the next man's," he reassured Whiting as the rancher's eyes drifted into the distance.

"Wasn't thinking that," Whiting replied softly. "I was wondering why you'd come today. I'd planned on letting 'em loose, you see. Clean the place up, load my saddlebags, and drop the pole on the corral. Waited too long to get out of here, Mr. Two Hats. If I don't get going, I'm going to turn into a madman."

Johnny saw that Whiting was staring at two white crosses, surrounded by a small picket fence.

"My wife would tell you God sent me here today, Mr. Whiting. Don't know if you're a believing man, but I think she'd have a point." Johnny studied the face of the young man and saw lines etched in it he'd not seen inside the barn, in the shadows. His eyes had a hunted look, as if he'd spent his hours on the run. Johnny knew what that felt like, but not the depth of Whiting's despair.

"Well, come on in. Let's talk." Whiting clumped to the porch and shoved open the door.

Johnny stepped back and studied the small wooden house, its wood weathered a soft gray, the porch running the length of the front. Someone had planted flowers once, and their dry stalks withered at the edge of the steps. He'd not take advantage of the man's grief. He knew what the horses were worth, but the house and land were beyond his experience. Maybe he could rent the property from Whiting for a while, until he could start selling horses to the Army.

Either way, he'd have his herd. When Mythmaker and Whistle came home, they'd begin their new lives. Harry and Hannah would be free to get on about the business of living without the burden of supporting three more mouths.

Chapter Eight

Noble sent three telegrams that day, one to the Indian agent near Fort Sill, asking if he knew of the whereabouts of a woman called Mythmaker, living with a half-Comanche man. The second ran down the wires to the sheriff in Salinas, asking if he knew where Mrs. Hannah Monroe could be found these days. The third, pursuant to Peck's request, told an Episcopal missionary where he could be found and that he was in no shape to ride. The third wire was the one that set Noble to thinking. So he added a note to the wire and signed his own name at the end of the postscript.

The missionaries who received the telegram didn't quite know what to make of it.

"We'll just have to deliver it. It's only right." Reverend Taliaferro hated traveling, but he'd do it. Donaldson was a good man, even if he had thrown his career as a missionary away to help the teacher on the

Reservation. Sometimes, when the weather had been bad for days in a row, Donaldson would ride over and discuss the intricacies of Aramaic with him.

"It can wait. He'll be over soon, borrowing some books." Reverend Taliaferro's wife didn't quite approve of young Peter Donaldson. She told herself her dislike came not from his Kiowa parentage, but from his ungodliness. What young seminary-trained man would pitch it all over a schoolteacher?

"This sounds rather urgent. The man says he can't ride yet, which leads me to believe Peter must have been expecting him."

Mrs. Taliaferro sighed. "Then go on. If you leave now, you can get to the mission school and home before dark, if you don't lose a wheel."

Her husband smiled benignly. "I wish you'd come. Mrs. Donaldson could use some company from a white lady, I'm sure."

"Mrs. Donaldson has made it clear she prefers her savage friends," his wife replied tartly. "Any woman who would marry an Indian . . ."

She hadn't intended on such bluntness, but tact was not her way.

Her husband was having none of it today, however. "Mary, this talk is most unseemly."

"If you want to talk unseemly, well, I can tell you a thing or two . . ." Mary Taliaferro rolled her eyes, her sun-speckled face too old for her years.

"Stay at home, if that's what you want. I'm going to the school to deliver this telegram."

Reverend Taliaferro's displeasure with his wife was

a rare display of temper. But he was fond of young Peter Donaldson, even if his start with the mission had been rather rocky. His shoulder broken, smelling like a savage, and with not a decent shirt to his name, he'd been hauled to the mission by the U.S. Army like a stray dog, claiming an owner that couldn't possibly be his.

But Taliaferro had recognized him instantly as fitting the description of his new man from the seminary. They'd taken Donaldson in, and all had been well until that Ghost Dance nonsense. Taliaferro had to admit, he thought as he backed his horse in the traces of the buggy, that Donaldson's dabbles in that mystic silliness had put him beyond the pale. Reverend Taliaferro had been almost happy that Donaldson hadn't expected the mission to take him in again. He'd come, however, to appreciate Donaldson's grasp of ancient languages, as they'd discussed specific translations into many a night.

Driving the buggy to the Indian school on the Reservation, Taliaferro wondered if Donaldson would explain the cryptic message. Unlike his wife, he didn't like to pry. But surely Donaldson owed him some explanation. They were, he hoped, friends.

He found Donaldson in the garden beside the small house, his shirt open at the neck, sweat pouring down his face.

"Good morning, sir." Donaldson leaned on his hoe. "What brings you so far from the mission? Not bad news, I hope?"

Taliaferro quickly reassured him. "No, everyone's

well. However, we received this telegram meant for you. Thought you should have it as soon as possible.'' Handing the piece of paper to the former missionary, Taliaferro studied him as he read it. His dark hair was even longer, and the blackness framing his face gave him a most uncivilized look.

''I didn't think he was alive.'' Donaldson spoke to himself. ''Thank you for riding over with this. Can I get you something to drink, lemonade perhaps? Anna's just made some this morning.''

Donaldson' wife appeared at the doorway at the sound of their voices. Taliaferro remembered that the couple had been married by the post chaplain at Fort Sill, not himself, and wondered if it had been the wife's wishes, or Donaldson's.

''Welcome, Reverend. How's Mrs. Taliaferro?''

Taliaferro managed to smile, although he knew the new Mrs. Donaldson was well aware of his wife's scorn for her new husband. ''Fine, thank you, Mrs. Donaldson. She sends her best wishes.''

Anna Jackson Donaldson smiled, but her eyes remained cool. ''Please give her my regards.'' First, she'd courted the disapproval of the white community because she'd started the school with no official sanction. Next, her crime had been that she taught academics, and not sewing and laundry to the girls. Third, she'd almost been run out of the Territory when Peter had shown up to help her with her students. Her ultimate crime had been in marrying him.

''I'll do that. Um, Peter, if you'd like to discuss this

communication, I'd be available. . . ." The name Peck had rung some strange bells in the reverend's head.

"No need, but the offer's appreciated." Donaldson walked toward his wife, tossing over his shoulder a quick "Good day, Reverend Taliaferro."

Taliaferro noticed there'd been no repeat invitation to partake of lemonade. Clicking to his horse, he drove back more perplexed than when he'd arrived at the Donaldsons'.

Anna watched the buggy leave, her husband sitting on the top step of the porch, his head bowed over the telegram.

"Bad news?" She sat beside him, her apron white against her dark skirt. She took his free hand in hers.

"I don't know. Remember the man I told you about, the one I brought with me to the tribe? When I first came back? Hunter Peck." Peter looked at the garden, but didn't see it.

Calmly she took his hand in hers, waiting for him to lead the way. She'd known him as a confused missionary, then a dedicated teacher. She didn't know much about what it had taken to get him back to Indian Territory from the seminary.

"I remember he left with the man the tribe sent up north to see what they were doing with the Ghost Dance."

Peter nodded. "That's the man." He fingered the telegram, rolling it into a telescope.

"I have to wire Peck I'll do what I can, clear his name and mine." He walked quickly, aiming for the small hill just beyond the back edge of the schoolyard.

The dirt had been scuffed to the hardness of brick by the children playing at recess. He wondered if he'd see them kicking the ball, throwing it, when the next term began. Anna followed him, keeping by his side. Finally, he seemed to realize she was still with him, and stopped.

He stared into her brown eyes, wide-spaced, calm, with a hint of apprehension in their depths. The dry grass under his feet felt like his soul, parched for the truth. She had not known the full manner of man she'd married, and he dreaded her reaction to his tale. But there was no avoiding it. She deserved no less than the whole, ugly story.

"Met Peck when I got off the train. Wanted to ride the rest of the way to the Mission, feel the wind in my hair, smell the land that'd been taken from me when the Quakers sent me east. Didn't have a choice, back then, about leaving. Had a choice, in coming back."

Anna watched her feet and the grass as they climbed the small hill. "Was it the right choice? Returning?" she asked.

Peter smiled at her anxious face. "I found you. Couldn't have been more right."

Anna relaxed, but walked ahead of him, as though trying to keep ahead of the words he was about to speak.

"So Peck took me under his wing, in a manner of speaking." Peter was remembering the moment he'd realized he was nothing to the white woman from whom he'd tried to rent a room for the night. As an Indian, he was lower than nothing.

"Ended up in a place I shouldn't have been, trying to tell the . . ." He wondered how explicit he should be with his wife about the soiled doves he tried to save. "Trying to tell the inhabitants of a rather unsavory place that God's salvation was available to them."

"That bad?" Anna gave him an amused glance over her shoulder.

"Bad enough." Peter remembered the painted lady who'd broken his collarbone with a kick. "Got into a fight, got hurt, Peck took me back to his place to patch me up. Later that night, he discovered the, um, lady he rented from was dead in her bed. White woman, called the Widow Eileen."

"What was he doing visiting his landlady in the middle of the night?"

"Anna," he protested.

"Oh, I see," she replied wisely. "I'm not so sheltered as you would believe, Peter."

He was embarrassed. "Anyway, he said we'd be accused of doing the deed. A half-breed and a full-blooded Kiowa, one of whom was rather the worse for wear and didn't own a shirt without blood on it."

"I can guess who that was." Anna reached the peak of the hill before him, and stared down with her solemn brown eyes. He'd never loved a woman as much as he loved her.

"Not exactly what the mission was expecting, a young seminary student with a broken bone received in a barroom brawl with several painted ladies and their irate customers. Peck convinced me my word of honor wasn't going to be enough to get us out of jail, much less a noose, so we ran. The two of us."

"Can't see you running from trouble," Anna whispered. He hadn't run from her, that much was sure.

"Not proud of it. Long and short of the story is, I reckon we're wanted men. Got to face up to it, knew it would happen one of these days."

"And that day is here." Anna spoke firmly.

"I would say so, yes. Peck's looking for me. Didn't know he was still alive, after he took off. If I can convince him to return with me, I will. If not, I'll do what I must to clear my name."

"Why?" Anna turned suddenly, staring at him as if she'd never met him in her life.

"Why what? It's the right thing to do."

"Run and pull a noose over your head? Don't be blind, Peter. You're still Kiowa, nothing's changed since that night the woman was killed."

"Never expected to hear you talk like this." Peter felt his annoyance rising. He'd expected tears, perhaps shock. But not this.

"You can do a sight more good here, teaching these children, than you can dancing at the end of a rope. Let sleeping dogs lie. Peck's the one looking for you, not the law."

"Where Peck goes, the law won't be far behind."

"Then stay away from him. You didn't kill her. You don't know for sure if he did, or not. Walking through a cow pasture is a sure-fired way to get cow

pies on your boots. Stay out of that pasture, Peter.''
Anna's voice was hard, harder than he'd ever heard it.

"I can't do that."

"Won't, you mean." She turned from him in disgust. "Men. Not a practical bone in their bodies." With that, she stomped back down the hill, heading away from him but not back to their house.

He had no idea where she was going. He hadn't been married long enough to understand a woman's need to be alone. Her suggestion that he leave the matter to Peck rankled, however. Of course, he hadn't asked her opinion; he'd told her what he planned to do. If she wasn't happy with it, she'd have to live with it.

What he really wanted were words of comfort, arms around him, reassuring him he was doing the right thing. He'd not get that from his wife, that much was plain as the cow pies on the bottom of his boots she'd referenced.

She'd been right about staying out of the pasture. But he'd been there, and the stink of manure wouldn't lessen until he could scrape this mess from his soul. He needed to know vindication, to offer his honesty as his badge of honor. She'd come around, he thought hopefully, watching her back as she strode across the prairie like a woman on a mission. She was a practical woman, and an honest one. Her ideals were solid and exemplified in the life she'd chosen, a life no other white woman in her right mind would have chosen.

Suddenly, he realized the source of their dissension. Her mission in life, the education of his people, would be ill served if he left her now to face a jury. He knew how it would look to white people—an Indian teacher charged with murder, a murder he'd run from and tried to hide. She'd made an imprudent choice when she'd wed him, and it was all his fault. He'd deceived her. Shame swept over him.

Racing down the hill, he was intent on his apology. He'd keep her out of it, if he could. The school too. Running until his sides ached and his breath tore in his throat, he finally caught up with her.

"What?" Twirling, her skirts caught in a gust of wind, she flared at him.

"I'm sorry, Anna. I didn't think what this would mean to you and the school. I promise, I'll not say a word. . . ."

"You're a bigger goose than I thought, Peter Donaldson. Do you think I give a fig for this school, without you? How can such a smart man be so stupid?" She began to cry. Tears were his undoing.

Pulling her stiff-armed body to his, he tried to understand. "Then what is it, my love?"

"Ohhhh," she wailed, hitting his chest with her fists. "Can't you see, I can't abide the thought of losing you."

He hadn't seen that, of course. "Ssshh," he soothed. "You can't lose me. I'm sticking to you for eternity. See this burr in your skirt?" He loosened the offending pod.

"Nothing can pull me away from you. Nothing. It'll be fine."

"Not if you go back with that Peck person, it won't.

I know trouble a mile off, and you're walking into it with your eyes shut.'' She snuffled loudly.

''That's where you're wrong. I know just what I'm doing. Think I'd do something like this without help?'' He thought of all his adopted mother, Mythmaker, had survived, all she'd done for his people. ''I'll contact my mother. She'll know a good lawyer, I won't go back until I know I have someone on my side.''

''Hmmpfh.'' Anna tried to stop crying. ''That's some consolation, but not much.'' She relaxed a bit in his arms.

''Peck's in Kansas, with my mother's brother. I recognized the name on the telegram. That's where I'll go first. I won't go back to stand trial, until I know I can scrape this mess off my boots.'' He chuckled for her benefit.

She sighed and laid her head on his chest. ''I can't live without you, you know.''

''I can't live without you.''

The day was winding down, and she suddenly looked very tired. ''Do you really think a white jury will believe you?''

Peter retained her hand, willing her to understand. ''At least I don't look like a ruffian now,'' he said and chuckled. ''But if it goes bad . . .''

Turning swiftly from his arms, Anna tucked errant hairs back into her bun. ''Don't borrow trouble, Peter. It'll borrow you soon enough.''

Their union was too new for him to read her as clearly as he would in the years to come. He prayed there'd be many more with her at his side. "I have to face this. Didn't expect it, but now it's here, it won't go away."

"I know that." Anna pivoted and gave him a small smile, and the gift of her blessing. "Do what's right. The school will survive without you, if you need to go away. We've got a couple of months until we open again, to do what has to be done."

His race had never been a matter to be noticed between them. Without the words to explain what it would be like to be an Indian testifying in court, he returned her smile with a false bravado.

When the federal marshals showed up, he'd be ready. His affairs would be in order, should he never come back.

"I'll answer this tomorrow," he decided. No sense waiting, trouble had come to their door and was banging furiously.

Chapter Nine

Harry'd left the winded horse the thief Gravitt had ridden behind. I'd wondered if he planned on any posse following the poor animal's trail, but at any rate, we didn't have time to wait for it to regain its strength. Gravitt had ridden the beast into the ground.

I was wondering what had happened to that horse as I flipped pancakes in the pan over the fire. Hannah's the cook in the household, but I can handle a flapjack. She was busy entertaining Whistle, who had reached the beyond-hungry stage and was cranky. We'd pressed on until night fell, hoping to get Gravitt to Larned before we ran into whoever was following him.

I noticed Harry listening to the night. I never felt alone sleeping under the stars, but Harry was edgy. Gravitt lay in the wagon bed, moaning lightly. The time had come to do something about the broken foot, but Whistle and his stomach came first. Gravitt's harm was his own doing, and my son wouldn't suffer any more on his behalf.

Feeling rather starchy, I gestured for Harry and Hannah. They pulled closer to the fire, eyes tense. Only Whistle was consumed with hunger of the belly.

"Mama, can I eat?"

"Of course, my love." I spooned some of Hannah's blackberry jam in the middle of the flapjack, and rolled it up tightly. "Now, why don't you sit here by the fire and enjoy this, while Uncle Harry and Aunt Hannah and I help the man in the wagon?"

He'd been beyond good in not pestering us with questions about Gravitt. He must have sensed that we were, all of us, unhappy with the situation. I was beginning to rue the moment I'd thought of tracking down my brother, putting us on this road.

"Yes, Mama," Whistle mumbled through a full mouth.

I winked at him, and he winked back like a child, batting both eyes frantically. I laughed and was so grateful for him I could barely stand it. But there was work to be done, and none of it would be pleasant.

Harry and Hannah gathered by the wagon with me.

"Harry, you'll have to hold his leg still while I try to cut off his boot. Hannah, you sit on his chest, if you have to. You hold the light." I passed her the burning tree limb I'd taken from the fire.

They both knew what I was about. Without a word, Harry handed me his finely honed knife. "What about a splint?" he asked softly.

"Use what we've got. Some firewood. Won't be able to tell much about what's to be done, though, until we get that boot off."

Gravitt heard us. "Leave it!" he snarled.

"It's going to get worse," I countered. "And if the boot's bad now, wait until tomorrow. We'll be slitting your leg to the thigh. Got to clean it up, see how badly it's gone."

I hadn't liked waiting to set the ankle, but we'd needed to put distance between whomever was chasing Gravitt, and us. Harry was right, Gravitt belonged to the law in Larned, not a lynch mob. I grabbed my bag of healing herbs from under the wagon seat and climbed into the wagon bed.

Harry and Hannah followed. If Gravitt hadn't been in such pain, he would have been a handful. But we let him know we meant business, and he soon gave up the struggle. My bet was that the pain was blinding.

"Harry, hold him," I warned as I uncovered the leg.

Harry and Hannah took up their posts as I started to saw on the boot. Pulling it off would have made matters worse, but I wasn't sure my attempts to cut through seasoned leather were any better. Harry watched me struggle with the knife for a few seconds, then grabbed my hand.

"Let me," he offered.

Gravitt's moans were rising, and I knew the boot had to come off quickly. Handing Harry the knife, I tried to steady Gravitt's leg as Harry gutted the boot like a deer carcass. Without the boot, the ankle flopped like a swollen fish floating on the surface of a pond. Switching places with me, Harry used both hands to steady Gravitt's twitching leg. When I checked my patient, I saw he'd passed out.

I should have slit the flesh to see which bones needed to be set back in place, one by one. But I didn't have the light or the tools to do what needed to be done. The shattered ankle bones protruded at grotesque angles. There was no way I could repair this damage by the light of a burning branch. As gently as I could, I used strips of my petticoat to bind the sticks to the side of the ankle, to give it some support. If he used the ankle again normally, I'd have been more than surprised. The binding of the ankle had pulled Gravitt out of his unconsciousness and set him moaning again.

Gravitt was biting a piece of wood Hannah had given him. In the pale light of the torch, I could see his dark face, beaded with sweat although the night was comfortable. The ankle and foot were swollen like watermelons.

"Done, Mr. Gravitt." I offered him a sip from one of my dark blue bottles. I never held with the use of laudanum, but I'd made my own sleeping draught. "Try this, it should help you get some rest."

"When can I ride?" he asked, gritting through clenched teeth and shoving my bottle back at me.

"With luck, in about three months, would be my guess. Even then, I wouldn't count on it."

"You're not goin' anywhere." Harry jumped from

the wagon, holding out a hand to help Hannah and me down. "Except to the sheriff in Larned."

"Well then, I'd suggest you get this wagon rollin', 'cause they're coming up fast." Gravitt spoke through gritted teeth.

For a second, I wondered whom he meant. Then I heard the hoofbeats in the distance. Night hadn't slowed down whoever was after him.

"Harry, get the horses harnessed. Whistle, come here!" Turning, I saw Whistle's startled face. He brought me back to reality. Quickly I realized we couldn't outrun anyone, not with a wagon pulled by one horse.

"We can't do this." I touched Harry, watched Hannah's worried face. "If they want him, they'll take him, no matter what we do. I don't want Whistle to see it."

Gravitt heard me.

"Get going! You put me here, you get me outta this!" Gravitt bellowed.

The sound of horses breathing hard carried like dandelions in the wind. My heart began to beat in a cadence matching the fear pounding in my temples, and I wasn't sure what we should do.

Hannah decided. "Get him out of the wagon," she snapped. "We can get out of here before they—"

I hauled Whistle onto my hip. He was getting too big to run with him in my arms, but we didn't have much time.

"Too late, come with me," I hissed, twirling to find a hiding place.

"I'll stay," Harry barked, his face pale in the torch-light. "Don't come out, either of you, no matter what."

He was playing with fire, but he knew it. Plucking Hannah's sleeve, I quickly shifted Whistle closer to me and ran for the shelter of the tall grass as far from our campsite as I could go, and still hear what was to come. Stuck to the ground like molasses on a dry plate, Hannah stared at Harry.

"Do as I say," Harry commanded, waving at her. "Keep quiet."

We had no way of knowing if the men who sought Gravitt were lawmen, or other bandits. "Hannah!" I'd seldom spoken to her as sharply. "Listen to Harry!"

My heart thumping, I tripped into a small depression and crashed down.

"Ooff," Whistle sighed in my ear as I landed on my back.

"Quiet," I ordered him in Kiowa. He knew what that meant. Every Indian child understood the need for complete silence at a young age, and Johnny had trained him well.

Gasping in surprise, Hannah slid beside us. I cupped my hand to her mouth and gave her the same command. Bits jangled as hooves thudded to the wagon. We listened, our hearts in our throats. I remembered vividly the day the Kiowa chiefs had stood before Colonel Grierson's front porch at Fort Sill and faced windows filled with Buffalo Soldiers. My husband was lost to me that day. I prayed Hannah wouldn't lose hers tonight.

"What can I do for you?" Harry sounded as normal as a man could sound, surrounded by night riders.

I tried to peek, but was afraid to rise too far out of our hiding place. But I could hear the voices clearly.

"Looking for a man, left a horse a ways back, ridden hard. You seen him, black skinned?" The speaker had the deep voice of a man who believed in his authority.

"Guess so. What's the problem, if there is one?" Harry was remarkably calm. I knew my voice would have wavered, if I'd tried to speak.

"Which way he head? On foot, or take one of yours?" I imagined them studying Harry and the wagon by the torch he still held. The team was staked in the grass. They'd see a gangly man with wild red hair, freckles darkened by the sun, hands made to hold a plow. But they wouldn't see the man who'd searched for long, lonely years for his wife, stolen by the Comanches. That man had more grit than they'd ever met before.

"Don't rightly know. Gave him some water. When we left, he was still mounted."

Harry, Harry, I prayed, don't lie. Walk around the truth, but don't lie.

"Where you headed?" This was another voice, suspicion not held in check.

"Larned. Meeting a man there. About some land."

"You always travel with a full-loaded wagon?"

Harry didn't hesitate. "Not always. Don't see as it's any of your business, though."

"Mind if we check your cargo?"

I hoped Harry'd had time to pick up the shotgun.

"I do. Now, think I've answered enough of your questions. How about answering mine?" Harry didn't give the man a chance to answer. "Why you in such an all-fired hurry, you'd risk your horses riding at night, catch this man? What you say his name was?"

"Didn't say." The leader spoke again. "Guess that's our business."

"Murdering thief, is what he is," a shrill voice piped in.

"Put a bit in it!" the leader charged.

I wondered how many men there were, and how many were out for the fun of a blood hunt, and not to bring an accused killer to justice.

"Well then, I suggest you get going, you want to catch him," Harry drawled. "Can't be far."

I tightened my arm around Whistle, holding my breath. Now was the moment when we'd find out if Harry's bluff had worked.

"Where you comin' from?" Again, the leader was dodging the issue.

"A ways from here." Harry was as cool as watermelon left in the creek. "Not that it's any of your business. I know you?"

I raised my head and saw the lights flickering from their torches. Johnny had said Harry became a changed man, riding those hard years looking for Hannah. He wasn't the simple farmer he let the world see. Another man had surfaced in the past few minutes. Silence answered Harry's question.

"Name's Monroe, Harry Monroe. And who might

you be?'' Harry knew men willing to lynch wouldn't want their names known.

I hoped Harry's finger was on the shotgun's trigger.

''Makes no never mind, who I am.'' The silence that followed was broken by the impatient stamping of horses who wanted their oats and a night without a saddle.

''We'll be on our way, Monroe. See you in Larned, we don't find him, you hear?'' The leader had abandoned all pretenses of civility, snarling like a dog with his bone at the foot of another dog. The shotgun in Harry's hands had given him a pair of aces, and the lynch mob knew it.

''Be my guest, I'm sure.'' Harry's coolness almost frightened me. I wondered if Hannah knew this man we were listening to.

Horses scrambled, whinnied, as spurs raked their sides. I counted at least six riders holding torches, racing into the night. For the first time, I realized I'd been holding my breath. My chest ached.

''Whistle,'' I whispered in his ear. ''Stay here, until I say you can come out.''

I scrambled from the depression, crabbing low to the wagon so anyone glancing back wouldn't notice me. Harry quickly rolled our torch in the dirt when he saw me. Hannah was behind me, copying my stance.

''Get back,'' he hissed.

I knew how these men thought. If they were anything like the troopers who'd chased my people, they'd double back when they didn't find Gravitt.

''Need to get going. Soon as it's light, and they

don't see any tracks leading from his horse, they'll be after us like ticks track a dog.'' My voice sounded unnaturally high.

''Going the wrong way for that.'' Harry was trying to sound confident.

''They'll double back, and you know it. We've got to get going, see if we can make Larned before they find us again.''

''What're we going to do if they show up a second time?'' Ever-practical Hannah was studying the man under our picnic blanket.

''He's not asleep,'' I offered. ''Probably unconscious. Enough pain under that hide to knock a stronger man out for a month of Sundays. My potion should keep him quiet for several hours.''

''Don't like their looks.'' Harry wasn't answering Hannah, I noticed. ''Got hangin' on their minds, can't see beyond it. We keep going, if they show up again. You and Mythmaker, take the shotgun and wagon, leave him with me. You don't stop for anything, anyone, not with Whistle, you hear? I'll stay with Gravitt.''

''We're not doing that.'' I'd run from the Army's howitzers enough for one lifetime. A few men with guns didn't frighten me, but I had Whistle to think of. My Magpie had been a boy old enough to care for himself, in the old days when the tribes had run from the U.S. Army like coyotes, hoping to live to fight another day. Whistle was just out of short skirts, even though he could fork a horse like a full-blooded

Comanche child. If the riders came again, it would be daylight and we wouldn't be able to hide.

Neither Harry nor Hannah asked me what I meant. I'd have left Gravitt for them like bait, hoping they'd take him and leave us alone. Harry'd done more for the man than he had any right to expect. Next time, I wasn't keeping my head down in the grass.

"Well, what're we doing here, jawin'?" Hannah stepped onto the wagon seat, leaning down to take Whistle from me.

Harry and I stared at each other and understood. I wouldn't leave him to face those men again, and he knew it. Johnny wouldn't have expected it of him, nor did Hannah and I. Harry turned to lead our one horse with solid leathers into the traces. I helped him in the dark with the buckles. Brownie we tied to the rear of the wagon.

"Comes a time, a man has to let it go," I whispered to Harry as he lifted me into the wagon bed.

"Tell that to your husband," he countered.

I wondered how he knew.

Chapter Ten

"I'll be." Noble studied the answers to his inquiries concerning a woman named Mythmaker and a man called Johnny Two Hats.

The first in his hand, from the Indian commissioner near Fort Sill, said that rumor had it the woman and her husband had headed for Kansas just before time for spring planting. The commissioner offered to make further inquires, if Mr. McFarland so desired. Mr. McFarland opened the second telegram, the one sent to the mission for Hunter Peck. Reverend Taliaferro regretted to inform Mr. McFarland that Peter Donaldson was no longer with them, and had left rather precipitously. He had, however, delivered the telegram to Mr. Donaldson.

Noble stuffed the first two in his pocket, and opened the third more eagerly than the first two. He expected to find Harry and Hannah Monroe easily. Frowning, he read the sheriff's response. A new man in the job, his predecessor having taken to his grave suddenly, he'd never heard of the Monroes. He suggested that inquiries be made of the attorney who had practiced in Salinas for many years.

That cut it. Noble rode home with impatience brewing in his blood like a young man eager to kiss his first girl. Once he'd started thinking about finding his sister, the idea stuck like lint to a sock.

"Going to Salinas," he announced as he pecked Rebecca's cheek. "Sheriff says he doesn't know anything, but the lawyer in town might. Figure I'll do my askin' in person."

"Oh?" Rebecca glanced at her patient, now propped in a rocker, his foot on a stool. "Any word for Mr. Peck?"

Noble turned to the instigator of all this activity. "The missionary says your Peter Donaldson left suddenly. Here, read it for yourself." He extended the paper.

"Can't read," Peck snapped. "Take your word for it."

Rebecca reached for the telegram. "Says he gave Donaldson your message. Nothing else. Cautious man." Folding the rectangle of paper, she carefully slid it under the Bible reposing on the mantel over the kitchen fireplace.

Turning to Noble, she knew there was no changing his mind when she saw his eyes. He'd looked that way when he'd told her he had to find his sister, before he came back to marry her.

"You're headin' for Salinas? Peck hopped to stand beside the rocker, steadying himself with his maimed hand. "Well then, take me with you."

Noble studied the half-Indian. "No need."

"Got to ride. Don't want them findin' me here. Not with you gone, your wife and children alone."

"I can fend for myself, Mr. Peck. And my children aren't helpless." Rebecca watched the duel about to explode between her husband and her patient.

"Got to make sure the boy's with Mythmaker. Then I can turn myself in. Been doing a lot of thinkin'. Ain't much use, all lamed up like I am. May as well get it done and over with."

Rebecca shooed the children away from the front door, where they'd come running as soon as they'd seen their father's horse ride in. "Scoot. Get on about your chores."

"Mama," whispered Eli, grabbing her sleeve. "I'm the eldest, I should go with Papa."

"Your father will do as he sees fit. But I'll tell him what you said," she whispered back. Perhaps Eli would be a calming influence, should Noble and Johnny get into it once again, she thought calmly. Her oldest son was level-headed, for sure.

"Whatever you do about your problems with the law is your own business. I'm not one to send an innocent man into a rigged courtroom, but I won't have my family in danger, either." Noble looked to his wife for support.

"I'll keep the boy here with me, until you find her, or give up trying." Rebecca knew her husband would have more sense than to argue with her. ''Mr. Peck's fit to ride. Not in shape for long days in the saddle, but it'll come.''

''I'd rather the boy came with me, if you don't mind, Miz McFarland.'' Peck was feeling well enough to show his stubborn streak.

''I've made my decision, Mr. Peck. That boy isn't going to run all over God and creation, with you not knowing if the law from the Territory's going to string you up without so much as a by-your-leave. No, Mr. Peck, you may depart if you wish. But Feather stays here until it's settled, one way or the other.''

''Best get some gear together, Peck. We leave to-morrow, early.'' Noble knew, if Peck didn't, when to stop arguing with Rebecca.

Rebecca studied her husband from the doorway as he led his horse to the barn to unsaddle him. She never liked it when he was away from home; it reminded her of the long wait she had before he came back to marry her. But he had to make peace with his sister and her husband, if he was ever to be whole.

They rode out the next morning as Rebecca held the small Indian child in her arms, teaching him to wave bye-bye and smiling for all the world as though nothing could go wrong. Noble turned to give her a last look, knowing she'd left unsaid much of what she held in her heart about him and his sister. But she knew as well as he that this was his problem to solve.

Peck rode gingerly, like a man with a sore rump and a horse he was afraid would bolt.

''Been awhile, I suppose.'' Noble raised an eyebrow at Peck, noting the way Peck held himself stiffly in the saddle. "Keep your heels down, you won't fall off."

"Won't be the first time," Peck mumbled. Then, more loudly, "How long till we get where we're goin'?"

"Figured I'd start with the lawyer in Salinas. Woman I'm looking for, planned on dressmaking for a living, as I recall. Her husband headed to pick her up, oh, about four, five years ago, out that way. Lawyer knows most folks' business, he'll talk if I pay him for his time."

Peck thought a minute, watching the well-fed rump of Noble's horse, its gray tail swishing early-morning flies.

"I'll be movin' on, soon as you find out where she is. Mythmaker. You and your wife, you get Feather to her."

Noble twisted in the saddle. Peck was looking decidedly peaked under his hat brim, Noble noted.

"Suppose that's up to you, but you might want to ask her if she wants to raise another . . ." Noble hesitated, stifling any derogatory reference to the Indian child she'd raised already. "Another child."

"She'll take him on. She and her man."

Noble reined in, waiting for Peck to catch up so he could see the man's face. "Tell me about him. The one with her." He couldn't bring himself to say the word *husband.*

"Half-breed, but more Comanche than white, I'd say." Peck wondered at Noble's question, but the man had been good to him. "Did the Ghost Dance with the Kiowa. Other than that, don't know much about him."

"Did she seem happy with him?" Noble didn't know what answer he wanted to that question, but it had to be asked.

"Seemed to be. Never saw no fightin', no ugly talk. I'd say they fit." Now that he thought about it, Peck realized he was convinced Feather should go to Mythmaker because she and her man fit together like comfortable boots in a stirrup. If they could raise Peter Donaldson to be a good man, their harmony must have been part of the mix that went into him.

Noble felt the walls in him crumbling, brick by brick. Who was he to deny his sister her right to happiness? If anyone had tried to separate him from Rebecca, he'd have killed him. He let the topic drop, forestalling any more rumination until he could see his sister and speak with her.

Noble and Peck camped under the stars, eating Rebecca's biscuits and cheese for supper. Peck worked his maimed hand; it was awkward at first, but he was determined to find a use for it. He still felt off-balance with the missing toes, but the rags Rebecca had stuffed in the toe of the boot helped brace him when he stumbled. Although his inner thighs ached from a day in the saddle, he realized he'd soon feel more comfortable on horseback than on his feet. The one thing he'd never feel awkward with was his gun. Without it for so long, he ached to feel it in his palm, test his accuracy after months of staring at nothing but walls. A rifle would be another matter, but he'd learn to compensate for the lost fingers eventually.

Lying on his bedroll, Peck stared at the stars and wondered if he was making a mistake in riding with Noble into a town that had a badge. He could light out, leave an IOU for the horse, and let the McFarlands figure out what to do with the child. Truth be told, he thought morosely, he'd almost gotten the boy killed after the Washita, in the storm that caught them unprepared. Nothing he'd ever taken a fancy to had thrived, and he'd be armless and legless before he'd let Feather follow him to perdition.

But the next day Noble picked up the pace, and it was all Peck could do to keep in the saddle. Finding Mythmaker would either kill him before the hangman could or whip him into shape.

They finished off the last of the food Rebecca had packed, and Peck had the feeling Noble was waiting for him to find game for their next meal.

"Don't have a rifle," Peck noted wryly as his stomach grumbled. "Lost mine, along with everything else."

"Take mine." Noble pulled the Winchester from its scabbard and tossed it. Peck dropped the reins to catch it in his good hand. Tucking it under his left arm, he snatched the reins back in his right and wheeled to the side of their trail.

"Meet you up a ways, whenever you get something. Have the fire going, you'll find it."

Peck knew Noble was unaware of the years Peck had spent as a child on his Cherokee father's farm, hunting and fishing. But that had been nothing compared to the lessons he'd learned keeping out of the way of the law. His long illness had used his body hard, and any reserves of fat and energy he'd once had were long gone. But Noble's test was what he needed. If he was to survive on his own, he'd better find out right fast if he could.

He followed some rabbit tracks, saw where a fox had picked up the same trail. Dismounting, he tried to tie the reins to a clump of grass, then gave up and dropped them. Resting the rifle on his left arm, he chambered a cartridge. Practicing steadying the barrel on his forearm, he sighted. His arm, still weak, wavered.

Disgusted, he rammed the weapon under his arm and took off at a slow trot after the rabbit. He'd drop where he fell before he'd show up with nothing but wasted ammunition to attest to his efforts. Running winded him, but he forced himself to control his breathing in ragged little gasps.

Then he saw the flash of gray, the white tail, and without thinking, took aim. The rifle kick felt good on his shoulder. Triumphant, he scooped up the rabbit and carried it back to where the well-trained horse waited. The rifle he slid under his pack tied to the saddle. Stuffing the animal in the bag behind his cantle, he hooked the wrist with the maimed hand around the pommel as he swung into the saddle.

He was going to make it. Muscles might scream after months of sitting, his lungs burned with the effort of running, his aim was still a tad unsteady, but he could shoot and he could ride. He'd give the law a run for its money, if they came for him before he was ready.

Noble didn't say much when Peck caught up to him. As they set up camp for the evening, Peck slit the rabbit's hide with Noble's knife. Peck understood that Noble knew he wouldn't have returned if he hadn't been able to kill a measly little rabbit. They ate in silence, the successfully hunted rabbit a symbol of Peck's return to some semblance of control over his life.

As he went to sleep that night, Peck wondered if Peter Donaldson's deity was watching over him. The thought made him uncomfortable, but seemed a reasonable explanation for his extreme luck in surviving the blizzard through the care of the Kansa, and finding refuge with the McFarlands. If he saw Donaldson again, he'd ask him if, when the preacher man next spoke with God, he'd put in a word of thanks for Hunter Peck.

Chapter Eleven

Peter telegraphed his answer to Noble McFarland not long after the Reverend Taliaferro had done the same. Unaware his former colleague had tried to offer some protection to him, Peter fumbled with the pencil as he phrased his answer to this man who was a stranger to him in so many ways, yet not. But he told the truth, that he would do all he could to clear both their names. He could do no less. Standing in the telegraph office, the sun hot on his skin, Peter wondered if he'd done the right thing in telling this man where he could be found. Returning home to Anna, he was unable to shake the feeling he'd committed a gross error in judgment.

"Supper's ready." Anna met him on the porch, and he knew she'd kept a lookout for his return.

Dismounting, he looked up into her heart-shaped face. She tried so hard to look plain, to attract little attention to the fact she was a woman. He'd seen through her disguise the minute she'd asked him if he needed help at the Ghost Dance, where he'd despaired of finding his true place among his people. She was the most beautiful person he'd ever met.

"Can it wait? Talk a bit, out here?" He wanted his words to move with the clouds, the wind, to a place where he wouldn't hear them echo within the four walls of their modest home.

"This isn't going to be good, is it?" She closed the door behind her, stepping down from the porch.

He saw no way to shilly-shally through what he had to say. "I'm leaving today. For Kansas. Telegram won't do the job."

She was coldly silent. "I'll come with you."

"No. You know you're needed here. If I don't come back . . ."

She wouldn't look at him. "Are you packed already?"

"No. Won't take me long. I'll take the horse, if you don't mind. Leave the buggy for you. Reverend Taliaferro will lend you a horse for it, until I get back."

"Nowhere for me to go. My home, my life are here."

He knew what she was saying, that he was leaving both without so much as a by-your-leave. His actions must appear callous to her.

"Mine too. But I can't say good-bye to you, Anna. This isn't that, a good-bye. It's just a small business trip. I'll be back soon."

Turning on her heel, she marched back to the house, pausing to ask only one question. "Will you eat supper before you go?"

"No." He couldn't prolong his leave-taking of her, or it would kill him. He bounded up the stairs behind her, careful to keep his eyes from her back as she busied herself at the cookstove, pretending she wasn't upset. She wrapped a loaf of her fresh bread in a kerchief, added some staples to it, and handed it, without a word, to him.

Jerking the carpetbag from under their bed, he threw in a few clean shirts, handkerchiefs, Anna's food. He had to leave, and quickly. He couldn't handle tears, not from her. He had to travel, and fast. If he waited any longer, he'd stay.

Anna faced him with a cold cheek as he bent to kiss her farewell. He knew her well enough to understand that she was giving him her hard side, so he could leave. He loved her even more for it. She stayed in the house when he hurried to the barn for the horse.

Saddling the little bay was done with his mind elsewhere. He tied the carpetbag behind him with twine, swung up into the saddle quickly. He didn't dare look back at their tiny house, the schoolyard, the school, as he rode out.

The rest of the afternoon was a blur. He worried about their garden, the roof shingles he'd meant to replace that day but had left sitting in the dirt, and the fact that Anna would be lonely. He envisioned her sitting on the porch swing, the red rays of sunset giving fiery highlights to her hair, reading a book after dinner. He hoped she'd sleep without tossing and turning.

Sleep gave him little respite from his own worries. He prayed fitfully, seeking to listen for his inner voice, failing miserably. He only knew he was compelled to find Peck, to do what had to be done to straighten out the mess they'd left behind in the Widow Eileen's house.

He traveled hard, walking when his horse was too tired to carry him farther. But he made Larned in daylight, and sensed he was halfway through with his journey, spiritual and physical. Much depended on Peck, but with or without the man, he'd have the sheriff in Larned wire to McAllister that he and Peck were in Kansas.

He headed for the lawman's office first, the logical place, he assumed, for directions to Mythmaker's brother's farm.

The sheriff kept to the old ways, with a kerosene light on his desk and an old hogleg strapped to his leg. Peck nodded as he watched the man swivel in his chair and give him a hard look.

"Might you tell me how to find the McFarland place?" Peter felt strange, using his adopted mother's family name.

"Might be I could. Who you lookin' for?" The sheriff's eyes were older than his face.

"Noble McFarland." Peter felt no need to elaborate. As soon as he got the information, he'd wire Anna where he was.

"Ain't to home. Can I help you?" Only the sheriff pronounced "help" as "hep."

Peter used his most educated enunciation. "I don't believe so, thank you. How can I find Mr. McFarland?"

"Have to ask his wife that. She's over to the mercantile right now. Just saw her there, myself, ten minutes ago."

Peter thanked him and turned to leave.

"You here about that sister of his, the one went Injun?" The sheriff's voice had taken on a hard edge.

Peter swiveled to stare at the man with all the dignity he could muster. "I don't believe it's any of your business. Good day, sir."

Out here, he looked Indian, no matter what. He didn't care, except that one day his children might face the same reaction he did. Still angry, he marched to the store where Mrs. McFarland was to be found.

In the dim light of the store, shelves packed with the goods of a prosperous economy, he waited a second for his eyes to adjust. Saturday, he realized, was the day for coming to town. The place was filled with women and men. Hat in hand, he stared at one woman, then the next, hoping he could feel instinctively which one held the information he sought without blatantly asking each one if she harbored a fugitive from justice named Hunter Peck. He had no idea what Mythmaker's sister-in-law looked like.

She found him first. "Do I know you?" Her bonnet hid most of her hair, which he could see was a dark red. Not young, she still had the look of a woman who was accustomed to being noticed.

Before he could ask her name, a girl carrying a young Indian child on her hip swooped up behind the redhead. "Mama, Feather wants a licorice. Is it okay?"

The older woman nodded to the girl, and produced a penny from her purse. "Make sure he chews and doesn't swallow it whole."

"Who is that child, who does he belong to?" Peter asked.

"He's mine." She folded her hands primly, one on top of the other, her blue eyes hard on his. "You have business with me, sir?"

"I believe so." For the first time since seeing the Indian child, he forced himself to think. The boy was too old to belong to his mother. "My name's Peter Donaldson, and I'm looking for Mrs. McFarland."

"Found her." She was still wary of his reaction to the boy. "What can I do for you?"

He tried to reassure her. "I'm here about Hunter Peck. Your husband, ma'am, wired my mission, well, my former mission, on his behalf."

"You're Donaldson?" Her incredulity was all too apparent. "I thought, well, that you were—"

"A child. No, ma'am. I'm the Kiowa boy your sister-in-law raised. I'm Magpie."

Her face shone suddenly, and he could see the beauty she'd been in her youth. "I'm so glad to meet you, Peter Donaldson." Pumping his hand, she turned to call out what sounded to him to be a dozen names.

Children from all corners of the mercantile flocked to her immediately.

"You must come home with us. My husband will be so sorry he's missed you." Shooing the gaggle of children to the sidewalk, she held onto his arm like a grand lady. The tightness of her fingers on the cloth arm of his shirt assured him that she was startled by his appearance.

"Ride with me in the wagon, you can tie your horse behind. I've much to discuss with you, Mr. Donaldson."

"Is Hunter at your place, Mrs. McFarland?" He couldn't forget why he was there, though he longed to find out all he could about his mother's white family.

She shook her head, looking down from the wagon seat. "Not right now. He's with my husband. Come on up, Mr. Donaldson. It's a long story, and one you need to hear."

He handed his reins to a boy who appeared at his elbow and did as she commanded. But first, he needed to know about the Indian boy.

"The one you called Feather. Is he . . ." He hesitated, not sure how to phrase it. "Is he related to my mother? To Mythmaker?"

Smiling, Mrs. McFarland shook her head. "No, he's Hunter Peck's foundling. Named the boy that. I've no idea what his real name is. He's part of the reason my husband and Peck are gone. They're looking for . . ." She shrugged, as though giving up some struggle. "For your mother. Please, call me Rebecca. After all, we're family, you and I."

He was silent as she backed the wagon up, then flicked the whip to move the horses out. If Peck wasn't there, he had to find him, and quickly. But first, he'd hear what Mrs. McFarland had to tell him.

She started almost immediately, after introducing him to the wagonload of children behind her. His eyes lit on the Indian child, but he couldn't tell the boy's tribe from his looks. He was dressed in britches and a shirt, giving him no clue by means of beadwork or quill pattern.

''Your mother,'' the woman beside him began, ''lived with us for many years, when she thought Johnny was dead in Leavenworth.''

The story was going to be a long one, one he sensed she was eager to tell him. He rocked in the wagon beside her and was carried by her words back to the time he'd been separated from his mother, from his people, by the tides of history and the U.S. Army.

He forgot to wire Anna that he was safe.

Chapter Twelve

The truth of the matter was, Larned was too far for us, with Gravitt moaning in the back of the wagon. With daylight, we had to stop so I could take a good look at his leg.

The bones protruding from his flesh told me things had gone from bad to worse in a few hours. The jarring of the wagon had shifted them even farther out of the torn skin.

"Mythmaker..." Harry stared at me across Gravitt's swollen leg, as though warning me to keep my opinion to myself. But Hannah already knew.

"Leg's got to go." She turned from the wagon bed. "I'll start a fire."

"We can push harder, get him to a doctor in Larned." Harry was still giving me a look that said he'd back any option I might choose.

"Then he'll lose more of his leg than he would if

I cut it now.'' I was thinking aloud. ''Bouncing around in this wagon is going to make the fracture worse. If I can cut it up to where the bone's solid . . .''

''Will it make a difference, in the long run?'' Harry, ever practical, was trying to give me a graceful way out. The posse couldn't be far behind us, I thought worriedly.

''No.'' Gravitt's moan gave way to coherent words for the first time. ''Leave it be.''

Would they swing an unconscious man from a rope? Or was part of the thrill of it seeing fear in the condemned man's eyes? I wasn't sure, but I didn't want to learn the hard way.

''We'll do it fast. No time to sew up anything but the main blood vessels. Hannah, thread my needle, would you? Harry, you're stronger than I, you get the cutting job.''

Gravitt swirled out of the feverish fog he'd been swimming through for the past few hours. The night had seemed too long by half, with his moans.

''Don't touch that leg, you, you devils!'' His voice rasped angrily.

''You'll die, if I don't.'' I palmed his forehead. The fever was raging, not a good sign at all.

''Harry, get your canteen. Hannah, watch Whistle, will you?'' Pulling rope from the wagon bed, I fashioned loops for Gravitt's hands. I didn't have time to knock him out beforehand. If he was lucky, the pain would send him into oblivion. Slipping a knot in the rope, I tried to work it over Gravitt's right hand.

He snatched it to his chest, and snarled at me.

"Listen here," I began angrily. But anger wasn't going to help. The man was out of his mind. "That leg's shattered at your ankle. No way the bones will ever knit back together, not now. Your only hope of not getting gangrene, if you don't already have it, is if I take the foot off above the break."

I'd seen and smelled rotting flesh in the Army, when I was a girl. The poison that spread from a wicked wound and took a man's life wasn't unknown among the tribes, either. The ruptured flesh, the shattered bone in Gravitt's leg, were prime candidates for gangrene.

"Let me die, then," Gravitt snarled.

Harry rocked back on his haunches in the wagon bed. "Man's got a right to choose," he whispered to me over Gravitt's body.

It went against my grain to give up. But Harry had a good point. Plus, time wasn't on our side, and I didn't have any left to do some powerful persuading.

"All right, Mr. Gravitt, it's your leg, your life. Whatever you did before you found us . . ." I reached into my medicine bag and pulled out the bottle of dandelion wine I used to help patients swallow a bitter herb. Now I had a different use for it. "I hope it wasn't murder."

I didn't give him a chance to answer. Tipping the bottle, I splashed the wine over the wound. Gravitt, surprised, took a few seconds for the pain of the alcohol to register. He almost jumped from the wagon, grabbing my shoulder as he twisted in agony.

"You . . ." he gritted through clenched teeth.

"Mr. Gravitt, it's the only thing I can think to do

to keep that wound from suppurating. Now, be grateful it's over, and try to rest.'' His hand was amazingly easy to remove from my arm. He was weaker than I'd thought.

Harry was already helping Hannah and Whistle into the wagon. I hunkered down beside Gravitt, ready to pour the rest of the wine into his mouth if necessary. I hated to feel so little sympathy for a patient, but the man was less than charming and certainly up to no good if the posse was any indication. Saving his leg, much less his life, was something I would do if it were in my power. But I wasn't feeling gracious about it.

''Let me die,'' Gravitt muttered again.

''No, Mr. Gravitt, I won't let you die. You may choose that option, but it'll be over my dead body.'' Lifting his head, I placed it in my lap. The wagon jounced on toward Larned as I rued the day Hannah had come up with her harebrained scheme to go east.

I wondered how Johnny was faring without us. Was he missing my body next to his in our bed, our son's cheerful smiles, our friends' good humor and kindness? I was ashamed of my resentment of Gravitt, but part of me knew it stemmed more from homesickness than his problems. If we'd stayed home, I'd have been free from this worry. But I owed Hannah a lot, and this trip had seemed a small price to pay to make her happy.

''How much longer?'' Whistle spoke to Harry from his perch between Harry and Hannah.

Harry draped his arm over Whistle's shoulders. ''Don't rightly know, boy. Just following my nose, get there as soon as I can.''

"I want to go home." Whistle pronounced his desire with all the firmness of the young.

"I do too, son." I could see Harry's slight smile as he answered my boy. I wanted to echo him, but such wishful thinking wouldn't get the job done any faster.

"We'll get to civilization one of these days, Whistle." Hannah weighed in on the other side, just to make sure my son wasn't swayed by her husband.

"Depends on how you define civilization, Hannah." I was feeling less than charitable at the moment.

"We should have gone on to Saint Louis, without going to see your brother," Hannah snapped. "Then none of this would have happened."

"Nothing says we'd have stayed out of trouble's path, if we had." Harry knew I hated to fight with Hannah. We'd been through so much together.

I reached up to rub Whistle's head, his shiny black hair warm under my hand. "Don't pay us any mind, son. We're all tired and grumpy, and need a good meal."

He turned to give me one of the smiles so like his father's, my heart thudded. "Me too. Hungry."

Hannah rustled in the basket for some of our provisions. "Here, boy, you eat your fill." She caught my eye as she turned, and I saw her unhappiness with our disagreement.

"Be full daylight soon, we'll make better time to Larned." Harry too was trying to make peace.

All four of us stared at the horizon where the sun

was rising slowly. The morning air was rapidly warming, and I shivered at the contrast in temperature. Too much was happening for my liking. I'd grown accustomed to the sameness of our lives, the regular rhythms of the farm. The thought of meeting my brother after all these years, Gravitt's disturbing presence in our lives, leaving my husband at the farm, all knotted my stomach until I was sure I'd never be able to eat again.

Whistle passed me a biscuit. "Here, Mama," he offered.

I took it from his chubby little hand. "Thank you, son." I knew then all would be well, and took a healthy bite.

We'd sort it out as it came, I thought. I'd done so, day by day, during my years with the Kiowa. Patience is a learned art, and I'd forgotten its lessons. Time had come to learn them again.

I was feeling calmer than I had during the past twenty-four hours when I recognized the sound behind us. I threw down the remaining bit of biscuit and swallowed hard.

"Harry?" Slipping Gravitt's head off my lap, I stood, shading my eyes against the rising sun. I could see horses coming up fast.

Harry tossed the reins to Hannah and reached for the shotgun under the seat. "Whistle, get under here," he commanded.

Whistle scrambled to obey.

"Gravitt, keep quiet." I pulled the picnic blanket over his head, willing him into unconsciousness.

They were around us faster than I could believe white men capable of moving. The ragtag men who chased Gravitt as though he were the devil incarnate looked like the demon's henchmen themselves.

"Howdy." Standing in the wagon, shotgun loosely at his side, but with the hammers pulled, Harry stared at the riders.

"You lied to us, mister," The leader snapped. His eyes dismissed me and Hannah.

I started to climb down, hoping to pull Hannah away from the wagon, but she shook off my hand. For the first time, I noticed the small cottonwoods to the side of the wagon and realized Harry had pulled the wagon into them. He was hoping we'd duck behind their protection was my bet, but I couldn't convey the thought to Hannah.

"Where'd the women come from?" A bearded man wearing a month of dirt and no sleep, barked from the back.

"We hid, last time you showed up." I wanted to pull all eyes to me, so Hannah could get down and take Whistle with her.

"Looks like your man there bit off more than he could chew." The leader's eyes were dark and hot on mine.

"Not my husband. We're traveling together, is all." I prayed Gravitt wouldn't moan. He'd been fairly quiet for the past few minutes. "My husband's scouting up ahead, he'll be back in a few minutes." I hoped my lie would shift some of the balance in our favor.

"Leave us be." Harry was edging to the side of the wagon seat, and I figured he was nudging Whistle with his toe to the far side with him. Then quickly, he shifted back to where he'd been originally. "Hannah—"

But Harry never got a chance to finish his words to his wife. I heard the report of the pistol before I saw Harry spin and fall like a broken tree limb in a storm.

"Hannah!" I screamed, my eyes on Harry. "Take Whistle, run!"

Bending and scooping in one swift move, she tucked him under her arm and jumped. There was nowhere to go, but she had the right idea. Flying off the wagon, I headed for Harry and the shotgun. All eyes were on me and the gun, I hoped.

"You've shot an innocent man. You'll hang for this!" I knelt beside Harry, hoping Hannah had common sense enough to keep running and not stop. Glancing out of the edge of my field of vision, I saw that she'd learned her lesson well when the Comanche had cornered her. She was flying into the woods like the hounds of Hades were on her heels.

They ignored both of us. A handful of men bunched around the wagon bed, guns drawn, staring at Gravitt with twisted smiles.

"Got him, boss."

"Must be quite a bounty on his head." I knew Gravitt had no chance of running, but I'd not let him swing without raising a few blisters with my words.

"Taking the law in your own hands died out a ways back, leastwise, it did in places where a woman and her children can be safe. Thought all of Kansas was like that now. Where'd you scum come from?''

All but one man ignored me.

"Haul him outta there!''

"Leave him be! He's hurt!'' We'd seen their faces, they'd have to kill Hannah and me to avoid our identification of them as Harry's and Gravitt's murderers. I pressed the tips of my fingers to the V at the base of Harry's throat and felt a pulse. At least he wasn't dead yet.

They ignored me, jerking Gravitt out of the wagon bed like a sack of flour. The pain must have been excruciating, but all I saw was naked fury on Gravitt's face.

"Let 'em have their fun, lady,'' Gravitt yelled as I stood, torn between staying to help Harry and trying to stop the lynching. I knew I'd fail at both, but I had to try. At least my interference, though no more bothersome to this mangy crew than the buzz of a mosquito, had deflected attention from Hannah and Whistle's escape. Though, I reasoned frantically, they could ride Hannah and Whistle down at their leisure, once they'd finished with those of us at the wagon. Their only chance lay in my stalling for time.

There were no cottonwoods with branches firm or high enough to support a swinging man. The lynch mob argued loudly over what to do with Gravitt as the prisoner swore at them with more strength than I'd have thought he had.

Feeling with my fingers for where the bullet had hit Harry, I found it. I couldn't be sure it had taken out a lung, but there was a chance he might make it if I could help him quickly enough. His shallow breath wasn't flecked with blood, not yet.

I tried to bring him to consciousness. "Harry, listen to me. You have to help yourself, wake up!" I chafed his hands and patted his cheeks.

"Harry!" He had to awaken, or we were lost.

The mob surrounding Gravitt ignored Harry and me, or perhaps I ignored them. I don't know which, I only know that the buzz and angry babble of their voices, Gravitt's snarls and curses, suddenly ceased. I applied pressure to Harry's wound, stanching the blood with my bare hands, as Harry's eyelids fluttered.

"Necktie him, drag him behind the wagon. He'll crack soon enough." The leader had made a decision.

"That's theft. This wagon belongs to this man here!" Leaping to my feet to shout at them, I could think of no other arguments.

They were bound and determined to break Gravitt's neck, but I'd not let them use Harry's wagon as the means of doing so. I stood, hiding Harry with my skirts, praying that Hannah and Whistle were running still, and wouldn't stop until they arrived in Larned.

"Well, we'll return it, little lady, soon as we're done. Just a borrow, is all." His voice was thick with sarcasm. I watched the sun hit the leader's broken teeth, highlight the dirt ground in the creases by his eyes. I'd seen evil before, and I was seeing it again. When they came back with the wagon, they'd kill me. Then they'd hunt down Hannah and Whistle.

I wished I had a gun. The shotgun had flown from

Harry's hands when he'd been hit, and I couldn't find it. I'd have shot the man before he knew what hit him. But I didn't have any weapon, I had only my wits and my words.

"My people are from Larned. They'll find you." My voice shook with fury. I hadn't thought of Noble and Rebecca as mine for a long time, but now I did. Johnny would never know what happened to us, I worried, unless Noble found him and told him.

"They're welcome to try." The head man's laughter was harsh as he let me know he wasn't going to waste his time bandying words with a mere woman.

"Stretch 'im a new neck, boys!" The leader's voice was like salt in a wound.

My only hope was to run while they were busy with Gravitt, to lead them away from Hannah. I could track her quickly, weighed down as I knew she was with Whistle. But I couldn't leave Harry, not while he still breathed. The air, warm as fresh milk, washed over my frozen hands, my face. Fear usually sent me into a hot sweat, but not this time. Silently I sang the death song. Today was a good day to die. My nails dug bloody ridges in my palm, as the gang knotted the the noose around the rear axle.

Gravitt twisted at the end of the rope necktie like a fish hauled to a river's bank. Cottonwood leaves clung whitely to his clothing as he mouthed foul words at the men who boarded our wagon and took the reins.

Like the rifle shot that felled Harry, the crack of the whip registered before I saw its effect. The wagon horse, startled by this uncertain treatment and rough hands on the leads, rocked in his traces. The wagon lurched backward, half over Gravitt's form in the dirt.

My voice wouldn't work. I could only pray silently, shutting my eyes to the murder taking place before me, commending all our souls to our God. My life had been too easy, I thought, in recent years. I'd been too content. The scene before me, the death of all those I loved, except for my husband, was my punishment for having found happiness.

The rifle retort snapped my eyes open. Frantically, I tried to see who'd fired it, if they'd hit Hannah or Whistle, or myself. I didn't feel wounded, but I knew fear and its rush in my veins could keep me on my feet for a bit, even with a fatal wound. No blood stained my body, and Harry still lay unconscious at my feet. Dazed, my eyes reddened with the tears I'd been trying to quell, I saw the man holding the wagon leads pitch forward into the dirt.

''What the . . . ?'' The ruffian beside him rose up, his rifle shouldered before him, as the other men tried to calm rearing horses and draw a bead at the same time.

I saw two men behind us, levering their rifles for more action. I screamed, hearing my voice as though it came from someone else. Whoever they were, they were going to shoot first, ask questions later. Throwing myself on top of Harry, I expected to be shot at any second. Which did I prefer, I wondered strangely, to be killed by men into whose eyes I'd stared, or total strangers?

Harry moaned beneath me, stirring jerkily.

"Harry, hush, we have to get out of here. Can you walk?"

He stared at me with glazed eyes. "Hannah?"

"No, she's with Whistle. We have to move, *now.*" I hooked my arm under his shoulder and tugged. Nothing. Harry weighed more than I'd ever lifted in my life.

The horse, bereft of hands on the leads, trotted forward jerkily. Gravitt roared as the noose tightened. Leaving Harry, I ran to grab the leathers, glancing quickly at the two men firing now into the posse. Their bullets showered the horses' hooves with dirt. They weren't aiming to kill, but the lynch mob didn't know that.

If I could cut the rope, get Harry to the wagon, we'd have a chance. But I had nothing to slice with, except my teeth. Lunging for Gravitt, I hauled him until the tension wasn't as tight on the rope. If I could get him into the wagon . . .

Men fired wildly, Harry rolled to his side, and I hung onto the rope as the wagon again lurched. Gravitt was very much alive, Harry was holding onto life. I would see us through this if it killed me. Just then, a bullet smashed into the tail of the wagon, splintering into my scalp.

The lynch mob had had enough. Valor wasn't in their vocabulary. Leaving their dead, they ran like rabbits chased by wolves. The two men racing toward us, chambering their next rounds, skittered to a halt beside the wagon. Shutting my eyes, I waited to die. Seeing

Johnny and Whistle in my mind, I prayed they would live long lives.

"Check out the man on the ground," ordered the man to my right. His voice was familiar.

I forced my eyes to open.

"Noble." My voice was barely working.

Staring down at me, his eyes widened suddenly. Leaping from his horse, he knelt beside me, lifting my chin in his hand.

"Sister? Elizabeth, is that you?" His hands pushed at my wildly disheveled hair, his thumb smearing the blood from my scalp wound away from my eyes.

"Oh, Noble," I cried, flinging myself into his arms. I was a child again, a girl with a brother who would always protect her.

"This one's still alive," said the man squatting beside Harry.

"His name's Harry, Harry Monroe," I sobbed. "Noble, his wife and my son are out there, running. Find them, before that mob does!" I could still hear the running horses of the posse.

Swiftly Noble cut Gravitt loose. I checked Harry, trying to stanch the flow of my tears. I saw my brother remount and ride in the direction in which I pointed.

"Harry," I crooned, "it's all right. My brother's here, he's going to take care of us."

"Thank you, Lord," I whispered, staring at the dark face of the man who frowned at me from Harry's side. He seemed vaguely familiar.

"I have a bag, under the wagon seat. Will you get it for me, please?" I had to tend to Harry, and quickly.

I didn't have time for hysterics. Gravitt would have to
wait.

I barely noticed the black man's limp as he fulfilled
my request. Harry's eyes fluttered solidly, then
opened.

"Thank you," I muttered as the man placed my bag
beside me. "Go and help my brother, please, quickly.
If those men should happen upon Hannah and my son
by accident . . ."

I didn't want to think of what could occur.

"Yes, ma'am." He mounted awkwardly. "You
don't remember me, do you, Mythmaker?"

Staring at him hard, I knew who he was. The awkward walk, the maimed hand had fooled me. Today, I
could see only wounds.

"You're Peck, Magpie's friend." I had never
thought to see him again on this earth.

"Yes, and yours."

He reined about, and followed a direction opposite
from Noble's. Hannah and Whistle would be safe, I
could feel it in my bones. God hadn't brought us so
far, to drop us now. They'd find my family. Then I'd
take us all home, and we'd not leave the farm again.
Not ever, I promised myself.

Chapter Thirteen

His place now, Johnny thought gravely. Owning land went against his nature, his beliefs, but he understood the necessity. Mythmaker would be pleased to have a home of her own, he knew. They'd make changes to the house as they grew accustomed to it, and to their lives there. He could hardly wait for her to return from Saint Louis. Now that he'd made up his mind, he was eager to be about the business of horse ranching.

Whiting had written out a deed in his own hand, copying the original and substituting his name and Johnny's in the right places. Johnny had signed the one-line promissory note, agreeing to send Whiting his money monthly to a bank in San Francisco. Whiting had pocketed the few dollars Johnny had given him as a down payment without even counting the cash.

"Good luck to you," Whiting had offered somberly, as though passing the title to Johnny was a handing over of an established curse. ''You'll need it.''

Johnny had hesitated, unable to say anything to console the grieving father and husband. ''Thanks,'' he replied, finally. ''I'll pay you regularly.''

Whiting had already mounted, touching his heels to his horse's flanks, when Johnny tried to reassure him of his trustworthiness. Johnny doubted if the man had even heard him.

Now he had to decide what to do first—head back to the farm, try and find someone to take over until Harry got back, or drive the horses with him and stay there until they returned? If he didn't take the horses, he'd need a caretaker for the ranch, and he knew no one in these parts. Driving the horses was his only solution.

He decided to lead the mare who was clearly the leader of the herd on a rope, and let the other mares follow. The animals would set the pace. He wasn't concerned about hurrying back to the farm, he'd left things there pretty well set, barring disaster. The handful of horses would be no trouble on the trail. In fact, he was looking forward to learning their personalities, their gaits. All he studied about his new herd would give him insight when it came to breeding.

One mare, a long-legged two-year-old, reminded him of Longwalker, the colonel's smooth-gaited gelding. Longwalker, dead of a lightning hit these many years, had been Noble's father's pride and joy. When the colonel lent him to Noble to ride in his search for

Mythmaker, Noble had been astounded. Johnny remembered clearly the sight of his friend mounted on the sleek, conditioned gray. Just out of boyhood, Noble had been both nervous and proud to ride the steed.

Noble. He tried to avoid speaking of, even thinking of his lost friend, for it only brought unhappiness to Mythmaker and pain to himself. Although they'd spent most of their boyhood together on Army posts, had signed on to scout for the Army at the same time, and agreed that finding Noble's captured sister would consume their lives until they were successful, their friendship had shattered under the weight of Johnny's love for Mythmaker. Noble, unable to accept his sister's choice to remain with the Kiowa, much less to marry a half-breed Comanche, had disowned her. And the friend she'd wed.

When Johnny had come back from the dead to claim his wife, he didn't even try to speak with Noble. Mythmaker had done the talking. Yet part of him always wondered if they would have been able to work out their breach, smooth over the angry words of so many years before. Leading the mare from the corral, Johnny sighed. Noble would have appreciated the beast. How he wished he could share this joy of new ownership with his wife's brother, the man he'd once called his best friend.

The idea came to him as he drifted, one eye open on his small herd, off to sleep his first night on the trail. The horses traveled smoothly, and he was making good time. With the purchase of Whiting's ranch and herd, he was on a path Noble could only applaud. Before Mythmaker returned from the East, he'd take a stab at mending torn fences with her brother. Whistle should know his cousins, his wife should feel free to visit her brother's family. He'd never paid a bride-price for Mythmaker. As soon as he could, he'd take the gray mare to Larned and find Noble's farm from there.

Decision made, Johnny closed both eyes and slept the sleep of a man with a world of worries lifted off his chest. The next day, he altered his course, and perhaps his life—his and his family's. He hoped so.

He missed his wife, his child, his friends. But forgiving old wounds would be a proper and fitting way to start his family's new life on the ranch. Saddling up the next morning, he chose a new path. He'd find out if the past could be healed.

Chapter Fourteen

Noble returned empty-handed. "No tracks I can find, woman on foot. Peck'll find them." He dismounted beside me and stared as though seeing a ghost.

"We have to get these men to town, quickly." I expected Gravitt to come down with full-fledged blood poisoning any minute. "They need a bed and care I can't give them out here."

My brother stared at me as though seeing me for the first time. "You've grown your hair."

I'd chopped off my hair when I'd been told Johnny had died, as was proper for a new widow.

"Of course. My husband is very much alive." I didn't know why I came out sounding like an angry wasp as I spoke to him. He knew Johnny lived. "Go, help Peck find Hannah and Whistle."

"Who's Whistle?" Noble frowned, his face more lined than I'd remembered.

He didn't know, how could he? "My son. Go, quickly, please."

Startled, Noble began to speak, then stopped in midthought. He'd grown more tactful in his old age, I was pleased to note. Ah, some aspects of big-sisterhood never left one, I observed with fondness. "Don't stand there, Hannah's probably hiding, and she's good at it."

Noble shot me an exasperated look, remounted, and headed in the direction Peck had taken initially.

Harry was grumbling to consciousness, fussing and demanding to be allowed to sit up. I threatened him with breaking off his legs if he gave me any more grief. The bullet, I found upon closer inspection, had gone clean through. This was truly a day of blessings, albeit some in disguise.

I wanted out of this cursed place. I wanted to go home, to nurse Harry to health in the snug little house we all had shared for so many years now. But I knew this wasn't going to happen. Rocking back on my heels, I felt the wind of change lift my hair from the nape of my neck and sensed that Gravitt had brought more into our lives than abject fear. All because of Hannah's desire for town life, we were on a path I couldn't see clearly. For a while there, I'd been sure we were all marching to our deaths. Somehow, I doubted we would ever be the same.

Fetching water from the wagon, I gave some to Harry, then Gravitt. My worry wouldn't leave me.

Maybe, with Gravitt deposited with the sheriff in Larned, I'd regain my peace. Perhaps my disquiet arose from the bodies of the men Noble and Peck had shot trying to stop the lynching that had me on edge. I'd seen violent death before, but it had been a long time. I could try to bury them, but the sheriff would need an identification once we got to town and explained what had happened.

I tried to still my mind by settling Gravitt back into the wagon bed and ignoring his ill-natured cursing as his ankle pained him. He, at least, was able to slide backward into the wagon on the blanket as I tugged it. He'd come awfully close to meeting his maker, but the experience hadn't given him a fear of God, not yet.

Harry would have to wait for Noble and Peck to do the honors. I couldn't lift him. I crouched beside Harry, packing his wound with herbs from my kit, my skirt soaked in blood—I don't know whose—and had to laugh. Maybe Hannah had a point about civilization, and moving east.

"How long could it take to find a woman and a small child on foot," I fussed at Harry as I tried to make him more comfortable.

"Don't worry." Harry patted my busy hands like a benevolent father. His voice, though weak, was stronger than I'd expected. "They're fine."

I batted at the grime and muck ground in my skirts, rocking beside Harry as we waited for a shout of recognition from anyone. Noble had been an Army scout in his younger years; I should trust him to find one woman and a child. I hadn't seen the lynch mob taking off after Hannah and Whistle, but then, I wasn't thinking too clearly at the moment they ran, either.

I wanted my husband with me right that moment. Johnny would find everyone, he'd take care of us, and we'd go home. I felt as close to tears as I'd come yet, and sinking beside Harry, I tried to tame my silliness. All would come right, in the end, I prayed.

"Hey, lady," Gravitt yelled, leaning over the side of the wagon, "you got me into this, you get me out. Get me on one of them horses, and I'll leave you and yours alone."

Staring at the wagon, I was sorely tempted. Saving this man had caused me all manner of grief. But something held me back.

"No way you're riding, and you know it. Just leave it alone, Gravitt." I hadn't almost died to give in to lawlessness now. The sheriff in Larned would have him, or no one would.

"Don't listen to him, Mythmaker." Harry struggled up on his elbows. "He won't be safe, unless we get him to Larned."

"I think my brother and that other fella took care of all this trouble." I swept the ground with my eyes, counting bodies. Fewer than I'd expected, but enough to make it an unpleasant sight.

"Met your brother, years back, when I was hunting Hannah." Harry was trying to pull me away from Gravitt's side.

"I know. You told me once, long ago." Truthfully, I'd forgotten the details. At the time, it had seemed to be another example of God's care for us, and I'd accepted his finding of Hannah as the first step in their path to the reservation. Once Hannah had found Johnny and me, the two of them had offered us the refuge of their home and a place to birth Whistle without fear of starvation.

"Was, wasn't it? So long, I plumb forgot tellin' you." Harry was floating, half conscious, half in the spirit world. "Seems like forever, we five been together. Another life, before that."

"It was, for all of us." I picked at the makeshift bandage on his shoulder, checked to make sure the bleeding had slowed. "Will we be able to go on as we have, Harry?"

His smile was twisted. "Not after this."

I understood. Hannah would either hole up at the farm and never go to town again, or she'd insist on moving permanently to Saint Louis. I thought of the calm oasis of my brother's farm, where I'd mourned the husband I'd believed dead. Did trouble follow me like a hungry crow? Would I bring it to Noble, if we returned with him?

"Where are they? Surely Hannah knows the lynch mob can't know her name, and Whistle's?" I thought I could hear Peck and Noble calling out to them.

"She's probably run to ground, can't hear anything. You know how she gets." Harry was trying to reassure me. I found it ironic that he was the one with a hole in his shoulder, and I was the one falling apart.

I was about to take off on foot and hunt myself, when Noble shouted in the distance, "Got 'em!"

I'd never been so relieved in my life. Running in the direction of his voice, I swore I'd never let Whistle out of my sight again. I knew Hannah would defend him with her life, but this was the last time she'd have to put herself in that position. From now on, those in trouble could fend for themselves. I was taking care of my own first.

Whistle rode in front of Noble, holding the reins as if on a jaunt with his uncle. Hannah straddled Peck's horse on the rump, looking hot, flustered, and a mixture of angry and scared.

"I'll take him." I beamed at Noble, reaching for my son.

"Mama, let me ride, please? This man says he's your brother, and he's taking us home." Whistle was calm, as always. Nothing yet had brought him bottomless fear, not in his four years on this earth.

"I need a hug, little one. Please?" I dreaded the day my son would think it unmanly to hug his mother. But that day hadn't yet arrived. I looked to Hannah. "Thank you, my friend."

She nodded, almost giving me a smile. Then she saw Harry and slid off Peck's horse so fast she dropped like a stone.

"Oh, Mama." Whistle laughed, holding out his arms for me to take him. Then he saw the bodies. "What happened to the bad men?"

"Got what they deserved, son." Noble glanced at my worried face first. "Don't you worry about them now. We need to get you to your Aunt Rebecca. She's never met you either. All your cousins are going to want to see you too. Got one about your age, I do.''

Whistle knew death only from the farm animals. I'd have some explaining to do, but later. Hurrying to Hannah, Whistle in my arms, I stood over her as she fussed with Harry.

''For heaven's sake, woman, I'm alive. Stop that watering pot falling on me.'' Harry pretended to be angry with Hannah as she gave in to her tears.

I joined her in adding wet drips to Harry. ''Thank you,'' I cried softly. ''For taking care of him.''

Hannah drew herself upright, tugged at her bodice, smoothed her grass-stained skirt as though it were made of satin. ''Got caught once, never happen again. You can bank on it.'' Her eyes flew to Harry. I knew to what she referred—the day the Comanche cornered her, when Harry was far from home.

''Is he . . . ?''

''Alive and kicking. Hope I got the bleeding stopped.''

She gazed at him like a girl with her first beau. Watching her stroke his beard-gristled face, I missed Johnny more than I could bear.

''Let's get moving. Don't want to be here, those men come back lookin' for more trouble.'' Noble was kneeling beside Harry. ''Peck, give me a hand here, let's get him in the wagon.''

Harry was weak, more from shock than anything else, I thought. Peck limped over to Harry's other side and bent awkwardly to help Harry to his feet. Hannah hovered behind him, trying to help. I could see tears still glittering her eyes. I hadn't seen Hannah weep in a very long time.

"Slowly," I cautioned. My bandage wouldn't take much jostling. "Peck, you hurt? Let me take a look."

I hadn't seen him shot, but he was clearly favoring one leg.

"No need, Mythmaker. Lost my toes, is all. Back in January, after Wounded Knee, Feather and I got caught in a blizzard. Some Kansa saved our lives."

Peck's twisted smile flitted from Whistle, to my face. "Got the boy outta there, afore the Army riddled his hide good, like they did to them others."

"It's a long story, Elizabeth." Noble waited impatiently by the wagon to hand me up beside Hannah. "We'd best be on our way, get the sheriff."

Seated beside Hannah, Magpie between us, I gathered the leads. Staring quickly at Hannah, I could tell from her stern expression that she wanted out of here faster than the team could carry us.

"It's over now, Hannah. We're safe."

"Hmmphf. It'll never be over. I don't care if this is 1891, we may as well be in the middle of nowhere, no law, no order, no sense of decency. . . ."

"Hannah," Harry growled from the back of the wagon. "It'll keep. Let Mythmaker alone, this isn't her fault. It's mine."

"That it is." Hannah twisted to stare at her husband. "And I hope you've learned your lesson."

Gravitt groaned as I flicked the leathers on the horse's rump, jerking the wagon forward. I hadn't meant to be so abrupt, but I had to get us out of there.

The smell of death was clogging my throat, and Whistle's eyes were big as saucers.

Noble pulled up beside me, as easy in the saddle as he'd been when still a lad. Farming hadn't taken the Cavalry out of his blood, I noted.

"Follow me. Peck'll ride behind, keep an eye out. Got a gun?" His eyes held mine. I nodded. I'd retrieved the shotgun, and made sure it was loaded.

"Noble?" I called him back as he twirled to trot ahead. "If I don't get another chance, wanted to say thanks. I don't know how you did it, but you saved our lives."

I was pleased to see he could still smile. "Just dumb luck, I guess. Peck and I were hunting for you. On our way to Salinas, trying to find out where Harry'd taken his wife. Peck knew you lived in Kansas with them." He cleared his throat suddenly, his Adam's apple bobbing. "Where's Johnny?"

"Not dead," I answered without thinking. Graceless of me, but I knew that was his real question. "Stayed back at the farm, keeping it going while we headed back east. Just a visit, you might say." I owed him the truth, so I spread it out quickly for him, like a woman who's anxious to get something out of her craw. "Talked Harry and Hannah into taking a side trip, so to speak. Wanted to see you, before Saint Louis."

If I'd kicked him in the gut, he couldn't have looked more stricken. "You mean, you were looking for me too?"

"Some coincidence, I'd say. Guess the Lord decided it was time we smoothed over this rough trail between us.'' The horse tugged at his bit, anxious to move out faster.

''Guess so. We'll talk more, later.'' With that, Noble spurred to the front of the procession, and all I could see was his ramrod back, so like our father's that I felt a lump in my throat as big as a buffalo. All was lost, everything I'd once held dear, all dead and bleached bones, I realized. My father, my people, the herds that once fed the tribes who'd been here longer than any white man—I sucked at the lump, trying to make it dissolve before I did. The bowl of the past was broken and buried.

Reaching over to Whistle, I squeezed his thigh, gave him a watery smile. ''You'll have so many new relatives to meet, Whistle, you'll have to take a month of Sundays to do it!'' I tried to laugh.

He saw through me as quickly as he could spot a prairie dog. ''What are relatives, Mama?'' He turned to Hannah also, as though she could help him.

Hannah shrugged, as if telling me this one was mine to answer.

''People who are part of your bigger family, Whistle. Connected to you by blood, or by love.'' I smiled at Hannah.

She smiled back at me, and I knew we were going to be all right.

Chapter Fifteen

‘‘**D**on't know what to do.'' Peck found himself mumbling to no one. He'd come back to the Mc-Farland farm, because there was nowhere else to go at the moment.

Then the younger Magpie was flying through the air into his arms, and he knew he was where he belonged. Noble had stayed in town to settle things with the law, a favor he highly appreciated, while he headed to the farm to tell Rebecca they were safely home. Mythmaker and her wagonload had stayed with Noble and the wounded men.

Peck had planned on leaving Noble's horse in the barn, speaking his peace with the missus, then heading back out on foot as soon as he could. He'd felt in his bones he had to keep moving, or he'd be permanently attached to the McFarlands and their brood. And to Feather.

143

"Whoa there, young'un." Feather had a stranglehold on Peck's neck. "Give a man breathin' room, will ya?"

Pulling Feather loose, he held the tadpole out aways and inspected the Indian youngster. McFarland food seemed to have gone straight into added inches, and chubby cheeks. Peck hardly recognized the lad who'd barely survived the storm with him.

The barn was dusky with day settling into night. The last of sunset streaked the floor red, where it leaked through the opened door.

"Help me feed the horse," Peck instructed the boy, waiting to see if he'd understood the English words.

Sure enough, Feather ran to get the oat scoop. "Good boy," Peck praised, patting the child on the head.

When he looked up, he was startled to see a man's shape in the doorway. The slant of rays framed the man, so Peck couldn't see his face. But his stance meant business. His heart beating wildly, Peck shoved Feather into an empty stall.

"Stay there, son," he ordered.

Limping forward, Peck wondered if the law had come to the McFarland Farm from Indian Territory. He'd left the rifle in its scabbard, and his hand itched for it. Part of him wanted to go down fighting, but the other part knew it was no good.

"You lookin' for me?" His voice, at least, was steady.

"I believe so. We have some unfinished business, you and I."

Puzzled, Peck halted, his maimed hand tingling by his side. The speaker was too educated to be the law, but there was a reason that brought him to the McFarland barn that meant no good for Hunter Peck.

"Let's finish it outside, where the boy won't be hurt." Peck kept walking.

"What do you mean?" The speaker turned slightly, and Peck could see his profile clearly. The man was Indian.

"Who are you?" Peck was reluctant to barrel past a man who might have a finger on a trigger. If he could get close enough to throw a fist, he'd feel a mite better about it, he thought wryly.

"Peck, don't you know me? You sent for me, didn't you?"

Finally, Peck was close enough to see the dark hair, the plain white shirt, the calm expression of Peter Donaldson.

"I'll be blamed." Peck wanted to laugh, to throw his arms around the preacher man. "Last person on earth I was expecting."

"Why? I got your telegram. Sent an answer. But I guess you weren't here to get it. Been waiting for you, Peck. Mrs. McFarland saw you ride up from the south side, sent the boy to tell you I was here."

Feather peeped around the stall door. "Hello," he whispered.

Peck hooted. "Got to teach you more words than that, boy, you plan on riding with me." He turned back to Peter. "So you came. Plan on headin' back to the Territory any time soon?"

"Thought it was a good idea. Since you're still alive, and look to be a daddy these days." Peter's eyes shone at Feather. "Like the boy's name, by the way."

Peck shrugged. "Didn't plan on takin' him with me, truth be told. Noble and me, we went looking for Mythmaker. Wanted her to raise him, since I didn't plan on livin' too long, way things are."

"I heard. Rebecca told me what happened, with the storm, the Kansa. Said you were a dead man for sure, but something pulled you back."

"Wasn't losing my toes, fingers, that's for sure." Peck paused, seeing a new maturity in Donaldson he didn't remember. "Still a dead man, and so are you, you throw your gear beside mine. Planned on a rope necktie down in the Territory, and that's the plain truth."

"Why?" Peter shoved his hands in his pocket, all his attention on the man who'd caused him no end of sleepless nights. The man he'd planned on becoming his first convert. The man who had disappointed him in many ways, yet still remained a friend.

"Like I said the first time, an Indian and a half-breed don't stand too good a chance with a jury down thataway." He was trying to be circumspect, knowing Feather was listening with eyes as big as saucers.

Peter understood. "Feather, run tell Mrs. McFarland we'll be up to the house in a few minutes. Go quickly, now."

The boy grabbed Peck's leg, gave it a hard squeeze, then scampered by Peter.

"Fatherhood seems to have changed you."

Peck snorted. "Not me. Just latched on to me, when his gramma died. Used him to get away from Wounded Knee, and he stuck like a burr."

"Not the way I hear it." Peter stepped farther into the barn, stopping close enough that he could see into Peck's eyes. "Way I hear it, you wanted to clear your name, so you could raise the boy in peace. Barring that, you wanted to make sure my mother raised him. Sounds like a father to me."

"Well, I ain't." Suddenly, Peck was embarrassed by his sentimentality. "Just tryin' to do the right thing by the boy, is all. Ain't got much chance in this white world, and you and me know it. Here, he'd always be that Indian brat the McFarlands took pity on. Wouldn't matter if he fit in like one of the brood. At least, with Mythmaker, he'd learn what lines he could cross, which ones to avoid."

"That he would." Peter ran his hands through his long hair, sighed, stared Peck in the eyes. He knew the direct gaze was rude by Indian standards, but he wanted to see truth in Peck's face when he asked him his next question.

"You really plan on headin' back, clear up that mess about the widow? If you are, I'm with you."

Peck swallowed hard, wishing he'd had the drink Noble had offered in the saloon before he headed back to the farm. But he'd been in too much of a hurry to see the boy. "Things got a mite complicated, preacher man."

"How so?" Peter frowned.

"You ain't heard yet. Found your ma and her friends, by accident. They'd been ambushed by a lynch mob."

"Where are they? Anyone hurt?" Peter's gut twisted.

" 'Fraid so. One of the men, name of Monroe, got shot. Your ma's fine, her and the kid, and the other woman. But they got jumped 'cause of a man they pulled outta the fire. Half-black, half-Indian, like me."

Before he heard the words, Peter knew what was coming. Someone else was paying the price of their sins. "Who is he?"

"Fella named Gravitt. On the run from this bunch of guns, huntin' him for a bounty on the head of a man named Peck, half-black, half-Indian, wanted for murder down in the Territory." Peck recited the words as if reading them from a Wanted poster.

"Anyone else mentioned on the poster?"

Peck shook his head. "So you're free of this mess, preacher man. Go on back to that pretty little teacher lady, I'll take care of this myself."

For a second, Peter was tempted. "No, you need me, Peck. I was there."

"But you don't know for sure I didn't kill her." Peck's words were chilling in their veracity.

"That's where you're wrong. A man who saves a child from the Army, then wants to see him raised right, doesn't kill a woman. Don't rightly know what went on between you and the Widow Eileen, but I'd put my money on you loving her.''

Peck started, his walnut-colored face darkening. ''Don't know nothin' about love.''

Peter smiled briefly, confounded by his sudden insight. ''No sense keeping the truth hidden, man. It'll save your hide.''

''Shows how much you know.'' Peck snorted derisively. Shrugging his shoulders, he seemed to give up the battle with Peter. ''Have it your way. Already told McFarland, when he talked to the sheriff, to let him know I'm here, and there's a warrant out for me. Left you out of the story. Up to you, what you do next.''

Nodding, Peter understood clearly the choice Peck was offering him. But he couldn't take the easy way out, not now. ''I'll ride in, soon as I can get saddled up. Want to see my mother, first. Meet her brother.'' Peter was planning on the meeting being their last. He couldn't see beyond the moment he let it be known he was with Peck the night the widow was murdered.

''I'll be here. Told the sheriff I'd stay put until he sorted things out.'' He didn't add that he'd just been thinking of heading out on foot, leaving the boy behind so he wouldn't get caught up in Peck's troubles. Unaccustomed to such kindness from Peter as he'd found with the McFarlands, he still found it difficult to admit it moved him. His face poker stiff, he held out his hand to shake with Peter.

Accepting the outstretched palm, Peter wrapped it in both of his hands and squeezed. Whatever happens, he was saying, we'll see it through.

He decided not to tell Anna that he'd had a choice, to walk away or stick with Peck. Somehow, he didn't think she'd understand.

Chapter Sixteen

" "They were in their rights, that man's wanted, sure as shootin'." Sheriff Thomas stared at the poster. "But you had every right to shoot 'em when they took aim at your sister here."

Noble rocked back in the chair in front of the sheriff's desk, neither relieved nor vindicated. What concerned him was the poster the sheriff was holding at arm's length, so he could get a good look without putting on his spectacles.

"You sure? That Gravitt's the one who's wanted in the Territory?" Seemed too much of a coincidence to Noble, that there were two men of Peck's ilk wanted for the murder of a widow woman in her bed.

"Says right here, there's witnesses, some as heard him boasting about slitting her throat and some as saw him trying to sell trinkets she wore on her person. Ear bobs, a pin, her wedding ring. Takes a depraved man

151

to take a widow's wedding ring." Sheriff Thomas shook his head slowly. "No doubt about it, that fella in doc's office is the one."

"Well, I'll be blamed." Noble hadn't spilled the story Peck had told him about finding the Widow Eileen in her blood-soaked bed, and taking off in the middle of the night before he could be accused of the crime. "So what's next, Terrance?"

"Get on back there with a wagon, load up them bodies. Gravitt ain't going nowhere, not with that leg. Feel like showin' me where you left them?"

Standing slowly, Noble wished he'd been able to leave the sheriff to clean up his mess so he could get home to Rebecca, but he was obligated to do his duty. Plus, he had to take care of Elizabeth and Hannah, and Elizabeth's boy. They were with Harry at the doc's office, fussing over him until the poor man had pleaded with Noble to take him back to the wagon, just to get him out of their clutches.

"Let me get my sister and her friend settled. Be with you in a minute."

Elizabeth would remember the way home. The way to his farm, he corrected himself. The farm was no longer her home, all that had changed when Johnny had come to take her away. She'd made the trip to Larned a few times when she'd lived at the farm, and she had an unerring memory for finding her way when everyone else was lost. Smiling at an old memory of her saving his and Johnny's hides when they'd gotten lost as boys, he was surprised, momentarily, that he'd thought of Johnny without rancor.

The doctor's office was behind his house, a neat clapboard affair. Letting himself in without knocking, Noble was surprised to see Harry propped up in a chair in the waiting room where the doctor kept his desk and books. Whistle played on the floor with a medical book, flipping pages so quickly they crackled.

"Hello, Uncle Noble," Whistle grinned. "Mama and Aunt Hannah are working." Groans came from the smaller room used as the surgery.

Noble glanced from the closed door, to Harry's white-lipped face. "Figured you were the least of their worries, did they?"

Harry's eyes flew open, and he nodded slowly. "Mostly lost blood, and a heck of an aching shoulder. Should be fine by harvest."

Noble nodded. A farmer knew what was important. "Can you stand riding to my place? Thought I'd help the sheriff back there, you know, the bodies . . ." He didn't want to press Harry, but he'd feel better if the man accompanied the women.

Harry's smile was wan, but still there. "Long as I just sit, and don't try to pull up the team, I should make it. I'm assuming you can tell me how to get to your place, and avoid you and the sheriff?"

Good man, Noble thought. "Sure can. That one in there"—he nodded at the closed door—"is stayin' put. Looks like he's the one on the Wanted poster, sure enough."

He was glad, now, that he'd kept Peck from heading back to the Territory and a mistake. That little boy needed a pa, and heaven knew, Peck needed the boy.

"From what I hear, the doc isn't too sure he'll make it. Hannah and Mythmaker are helping him take off the foot, right now."

Noble grimaced. But Gravitt's problems were of his own making, and he felt responsible for Harry, not the wanted man. "Tell you what, knowing my sister, she won't leave here until the doc's good and done. How about I get someone here in town to drive you and your wife back to my place? Take the tadpole with you. Hungry, son?"

Whistle looked up at the mention of food, and nodded vigorously.

Noble rubbed the stubble on his chin. He'd like nothing better than to drive the wagon himself, but he had to see this through. Maybe he'd have a chance to talk to his sister in private. The words would have to be said, sooner or later.

"Sounds right by me." Harry tried to stand, wobbled, sat down hard. "Thought I'd make it under my own steam, but it's been a long day."

Noble stared at the tall, redheaded man. The last time he'd seen the farmer, he'd been on the trail so long, he'd lost the look of a man of the land. Then, Harry'd been terrified the rumors of a white woman killed with some raiding Comanche would lead him to his wife's pickled head. A few years had passed between then and now, but even with the wound, Harry looked contented.

"I'll get your wife. You stay put until I come and get you." Noble paused, his hand on the knob of the surgery. "Harry, I'm glad you made it."

Harry's eyes were shut. ''Me too. When I feel a mite better, you'll have to tell me what you're planting these days.''

Noble chuckled. Farmers to the core, he and Harry understood the worth of good land and a good woman. His smile, however, disappeared as soon as he peeked his head around the door. Hannah and his sister, clad in aprons like the one the doctor wore, were holding Gravitt's twitching limb as the doctor tried to sew up what was left of it.

Noble turned his eyes away. Elizabeth caught him from the corner of her eye and tried to shoo him from the doorway.

''Need Hannah to help Harry get home. To my farm, I mean. He's about had it for today.'' Noble spoke to the wall. He could stand blood and damage as well as the next man, but it seemed obscene to study on this doomed man's misery. ''Your boy could probably stand a soft bed and a good meal about now too.'' If he knew anything about women, it was that their children came first.

''Hannah, he's right. Harry and Whistle need you. The doctor and I can go it alone from here on out.'' Mythmaker's eyes shoved at her friend.

Reluctantly Hannah relinquished her hold on Gravitt's leg and stepped back. ''You sure?''

''Go on, woman,'' Dr. Zekor snapped. ''Take care of your husband.'' He never looked up. ''Noble, tell your wife to feed that man out there lots of her good chicken soup. Needs to build up his blood.''

Noble smiled wryly, thinking of Rebecca, a born

healer, taking advice from the doctor. "She'll take good care of him," he promised solemnly. "Hannah?"

Dropping the stained apron on the floor, Hannah made an attempt to be polite as Noble slid the door open farther for her to exit. Just inside the anteroom, she rested her hand on his arm and cleared her throat.

"It's been a long time, but you're still the man who led my husband to me. And took care of me, when the Army had no more use for us." She referred to the days when she and Elizabeth had been held by the Army, after the Kiowa had been tried for stealing the mules and killing the skinners. "I don't know if I rightly thanked you. After today, seems I owe you even more than some belated gratitude."

"Long time ago, Hannah." Noble stooped beside Harry, lifting the man's good arm over his shoulder. "No need to ride a trail that's long gone cold." He faced Harry. "Hold on, friend. Hannah, let him lean on you, if he has a need. Don't think so, not with that bad shoulder."

Carefully, he negotiated Harry's way out of the doctor's office. The wagon, with a fresh team, waited outside. "Took your horses to the livery. Send one of my boys back to get 'em, after they've had a chance to feed and rest up."

Hannah hurried to hold the team steady as Noble readied Harry to get him into the seat.

Harry relaxed against his side. "Thanks." He cleared his throat carefully, as though it too hurt.

"What about back there? You need me to speak to the sheriff?"

"No need. It's all taken care of. That one"—Noble nodded at the office—"was wanted in the Territory. Seems those bounty hunters had a claim to him, all right. But they had no right to shoot you, and almost kill the women and the boy." Noble tried to keep a lid on his temper, but the thought still infuriated him. "Speaking of the boy, I'd best fetch him."

Noble got Harry settled, leaning against Hannah in the wagon, then carried a sleepy Whistle from the sofa in the doctor's anteroom. The child was stocky, like Johnny, but with Elizabeth's pale blue eyes. Noble cradled the boy's head in his hand as he leaned down to settle him in the wagon bed. His nephew. His sister's child by the half-breed she'd chosen over her own kind. Somehow, the thought didn't stir up the ancient anger he'd banked years ago. This was just a boy, and from the heft of him, a sturdy one at that. Noble was too experienced a father not to appreciate a healthy child.

He found more than enough takers to show the Monroes and the boy the way to his farm. The story of the morning's deed had spread through town, and everyone wanted to hear what had really happened. He brushed off all questions, accepting the farrier's offer to drive the wagon. A solid, large-armed man, Joe Langly wouldn't gossip about the dark-haired boy with Indian blood sleeping in the wagon bed.

After they were on the road, Noble stopped back at the doctor's office to tell his sister he'd return for her

when the task with the dead men on the trail was finished. Strangely, he felt no remorse for the killing,
although it had been a long time since he'd aimed to
take a man's life. The thought of what they'd been
about to do to his sister still made his blood burn. No
matter that she'd been lost to him for many a year
now, she was still a McFarland. She was still Elizabeth, the sister he'd promised their father he'd protect.

Watching her calm work with the doctor from a
crack in the door, he wondered that she'd changed so
little. Her face and hands were unfashionably dark, as
if she never wore a bonnet or stayed in the shade. But
then, she'd been that way as a child. Their father had
sent her east to a boarding school, hoping she'd come
back a proper lady. Her face, now tense with concentration, was more lined, but aging with a handsome-
ness more fashionable women would never know. As
she steadied Gravitt, adding a drop of liquid to the rag
she pressed to his face when he began to twitch, she
glanced at Noble with a warm smile.

"Take care of my son," she whispered. "And thank
you for his life."

Embarrassed, he nodded, pulling the door shut.
They'd talk later, he promised himself.

He wasn't looking forward to cleaning up the mess
in the cottonwoods. But it had to be done, so he could
get home to Rebecca and their children. Half his questions answered by his sister's presence in Larned, he
wanted more than anything to tell his wife that he'd
made up his mind to treat her to a trip to Saint Louis,
or even Chicago. They'd lived all their married life on

the farm, it was high time they kicked up their heels and had a honeymoon. The older boys could run the farm, and his eldest daughter, married and living on adjoining land, would see to the youngest children. That morning had taught him a lesson he'd learned while scouting for the Army, one he'd forgotten for a while. Life was too short, a happy one too rare, to squander with petty grievances and old anger. Rebecca had never forgotten that truth, and he wanted to prove to her that he too remembered it now.

Lost in his thoughts as he and Sheriff Thomas accompanied the undertaker's wagon, he was slowly aware that he was feeling edgy. The bounty hunters were long gone, the sheriff figured, knowing their man was a lost cause. They wouldn't want to return to face charges for shooting Harry, either.

"You feel that, Terrance?" Noble twisted in the saddle to face the sheriff. "Something's spookin' the horses."

Sure enough, tails up, noses to the wind, the lot of them were ready to pick up hooves and skedaddle.

"They hear something we can't." The sheriff pulled out his Winchester. "Might've guessed wrong, about them men."

Noble followed suit as the undertaker's assistant, a raw-boned boy, reined up, allowing the men to ride ahead. The wagon team fidgeted, tossing their bits as though ready to shoot off down the road, dragging the wagon behind like so much trash.

"Let's get to the side, see what's coming before it sees us," Noble suggested, reining to the right.

This strange day was taking another turn, and he didn't like it. Just when he'd settled in his mind that he was going to straighten out some old wrongs, more trouble was coming down the road faster than hail in a tornado. He'd felt the same tingling when he'd seen Elizabeth and the wagon, Gravitt's body flopping like a tortured dog on the end of a rope. He wished Peck were with him now, and not the undertaker's assistant. Bad luck, having the undertaker's wagon with them.

A soft summer's wind sang by Noble's ears. Annoyed, he swatted at some gnats that came with the breeze, and squinted at the horizon. Sheriff Terrance Thomas, on the opposite side from him, reined up beside the wagon and the undertaker's boy, frowning at the gentle hiss of wind.

His ears aching with the effort to hear how many the three of them would have to face, Noble shut his eyes. He'd stayed out of trouble's way for so long now, since he'd left the Army and scouting, he was out of practice. But his instincts to survive, like a welcomed old friend, had returned with a clarity, a sharpness, he could taste on his tongue.

His sister must have tasted in her mouth the same sharp will to live when the Kiowa took her. Eyes shut, he saw the bodies lined up under Army tarps, the women who'd been shot by troopers rather than suffer the ravages of capture by the Kiowa. Elizabeth had taken the riskier route; she'd chosen to survive. Suddenly, he understood her as he hadn't been able to when he was younger and had been a man without a wife and children to live for.

Sliding his Smith and Wesson from its holster, he rested the old revolver on his thigh, trigger finger ready. He knew now that they heard horses, a lot of them, moving at a steady trot. His old scout instincts guessed about ten head, traveling light, traveling steady. The undertaker's boy should make a break for it, he thought.

"We're outgunned," Terrance muttered.

"Was before. They aren't expecting us, not here, not so soon." He'd had the element of surprise when he'd saved his sister from the vigilantes.

"Maybe they just came back to collect their dead."

Noble didn't think so, but it didn't hurt to hope. But the sound grew steadier, like a wind aiming for the barn, and he knew the roof would be the next to go. Nothing for it but to wait and be ready.

A man riding easy in the saddle, a long-necked mare on a rope beside him, swung over the small crest of the hill where Noble gazed as if expecting the Grim Reaper himself. Scattered around beside him was a small herd, raising dust. Noble studied the horses first, noting that they were none of them very old or very winded, then the lone man.

He forked the horse like a rider who was more at home on horseback than on his own two feet. Hat pulled low, his eyes steady on Noble, the sheriff, then the undertaker's wagon, he said something to the herd, leaned back in the saddle to slow his mount, and gradually worked the horses to a walk. Noble was impressed. He'd seen men who thought like horses, could understand every twitch of an ear, every shake of a tail, and speak back in an unspoken tongue the animals could interpret as well. But all those men had been Indian.

The horseman halted a hundred feet away, the herd milling around him, dropping noses to search for grass. Noble and the sheriff spurred forward, still unsure of who this man might be, of where he was taking a herd no one they knew was expecting in Larned.

"Howdy. Seen any trouble on the road, stranger?" Sheriff Terrance cleared the worry from his throat, and sounded every bit as iron-jawed as he looked.

"None I couldn't handle. Might I ask, were you expecting some, heading my way?" The horseman nudged his bay forward a mite, giving the mare some rope to snuffle the ground beside the other horses.

"Seen any riders, men out for trouble?" Noble knew this man would understand. He rode with his gun ready. Noble wished he could see more of his face under his low-brimmed hat.

"Not yet. But the horses have been spooked."

Familiarity tugged at Noble like an incipient sneeze. "Do I know you, stranger?"

Terrance frowned. "Ain't seen the likes of him, not in these parts," he murmured.

The undertaker's boy knew enough to keep his mouth shut. Watching the three men size each other up, he was out of his league.

The horseman nudged the bay with a slight pressure of his heels, swinging sideways to give Noble a full view of his face under the broad-brimmed hat. Noble felt air sucked from his lungs like lightening had hit the ground beside him. He half-expected his hat to fly from his head.

"Johnny."

The horseman nodded. "Noble. How are you?"

Noble was unable to answer, questions swirling around his head like a swarm of bees. Words wouldn't work for him, not at that second. Touching his hat with his hand, he holstered the Smith and Wesson.

He tried to speak, found gravel in his craw instead. Harrumphing loudly, he tried again.

"Terrance, this here's a friend. My sister's husband."

Sheriff Thomas stared wide-eyed as a girl at her first county fair, from Noble to Johnny, then back again.

"If that don't beat all," he finally managed to reply.

Clear as daylight, Noble's brother-in-law was an Indian.

Chapter Seventeen

They loaded the bodies in the undertaker's wagon. Noble explained to Johnny what had happened with the vigilantes, and that Harry was on his way, albeit worse for the wear, to his farm, with Hannah and Whistle in tow. Quickly he explained that Elizabeth was in town still, helping the doctor. Johnny said little, his face as tight as a drum, as they remounted. The sheriff nodded to Noble and Johnny and accompanied the undertaker's boy to town.

Johnny and Noble stared at each other, the horses calmly grazing nearby.

"Fine herd." Noble broke the silence first.

"That it is. Bought it from a man down south, his ranch too." Johnny found it strange the two of them could converse so serenely after all the years of deafening silence.

"That's good. Elizabeth didn't say anything about it."

"She doesn't know yet." Johnny's smile was wary.

"My oh my. Don't think I'd like to be in your shoes." Noble understood, like any long-time husband, that wives didn't like surprises when it came to major purchases.

"Not sure I want to be in 'em, either." Johnny laughed.

The silence between them was interrupted by the impatient stomping of horse hooves as the animals pawed for juicy morsels to chew.

"Thought of you, when I saw the gray." Nodding at the herd, Johnny nudged his horse closer to the horse under discussion.

Noble followed, eyes narrowed. "Well, I'll be. Never thought I'd see a horse like Longwalker, not again."

"That's what I thought. Same pasterns, bit smaller, but balanced like he was." Johnny hesitated. "Thought you might like to have him."

Noble's throat clogged. His head nodding quickly, he accepted the peace offering. "Looks like they're unbroken."

"Sure are. Fella that raised 'em didn't have the heart to rough-break 'em. Figured I could use some help. Don't know a man who thinks like I do about horses, 'cept you, Noble." Johnny cleared his throat. "Thought we could work out a deal; I'll raise the herd, we'll get them under saddle, you do the sellin'. Army still buying?''

Noble thought a minute. ''Got a wagonload of boys, back at the farm. About time they learned some horse sense.''

''Sounds good to me. My son's a mite young to be riding anything this green.''

Noble shoved his hat back on his head and smiled with genuine warmth. ''Fine-looking boy you've got there, Johnny.'' He went to the heart of the matter. ''Elizabeth seems to be, well, herself. Time hasn't changed her much, has it?''

Johnny grinned again. ''Nothing can change a woman that stubborn.''

His old friend returned the smile, knowing now they could let bygones be bygones. ''That she is. Almost as pigheaded a woman as my Rebecca.'' Noble's eyes turned sad. ''It's been a long time, Johnny.''

Nodding, Johnny held out his hand across his horse's withers. ''Too long.''

They shook hands, sealing a silent bargain.

''Well, we'd best get these fine-lookin' animals to some grain.'' For the first time in years, Noble felt his eyes misting over. ''Your wife and son'll be happy to see you.'' He didn't hesitate using the word *wife*.

''Well, we'll see how that goes, when I explain to her about the ranch. Don't know yet how I'm going to tell the Monroes we'll be packin' up and leavin'.'' Johnny handed Noble the rope for the mare, then began to circle the herd to pull them together.

''Good golly, you'll be wanting to get this herd put

to bed.'' Noble smacked his hand against his thigh. ''I'll fetch Elizabeth, bring her to the farm, when she's ready to leave the doc.''

''I'll get her. Give me a chance to explain, before we see the Monroes. Think you can drive the herd alone?''

''Shoot, you did it. Think I've lost my touch?'' Noble snorted. He didn't think he wanted to witness what would happen when Johnny started his explanations.

''Wouldn't be here, thought that. Question is, how do I find my wife?''

''Easier than finding her when she was taken, off that Army transport.'' As soon as he said the words, Noble was glad he'd made a small joke about the event that had driven the wedge in their friendship. ''Look for the doc's house, south end of town. White clapboard, black shutters. Office out back, she should be there.''

Johnny sat his horse, unmoving. ''Can't say I'm lookin' forward to this.''

''Don't blame you.'' Noble chuckled. ''Wouldn't be in your shoes for all the horses in these United States.''

''She'll be happy about it. The ranch.'' Johnny squared his shoulders, as if about to face a firing squad. ''She'll be right pleased.'' Aiming for Larned, he kept to a slow walk. Twisting to raise a hand in farewell, he smiled. ''May have to stay with you, when she throws me out.''

''You'll be welcome. Go on, get it done and over with.'' Noble began herding the horses. ''Bring the

Monroes' team, when you leave town. They're at the livery.''

Johnny gave another small wave and showed Noble his squared back. This was going to be one of the toughest things he'd ever had to do. Marrying Mythmaker, alienating Johnny, had been hard but something he'd had to do. This ranch was all his choice, and she'd had no say in it. The longer it took to get to her, the less he thought of his good idea.

Trying to avoid the dread growing inside him like a meal gone bad, he turned to his memories. He remembered the last time he'd been here, when he'd come to claim his wife. Their long years apart had melted like a lit candle in a breeze. The years since they'd begun their marriage anew had been, overall, good. They hadn't seen eye-to-eye on everything, but one or the other of them had always given ground when necessary. The four years with the Monroes had been his biggest concession. Somehow, he doubted if his wife saw it that way.

He was Comanche. Horses were in his blood. They'd be in his son's blood also. He didn't want his boy to grow up to be a tiller of the earth. If Hannah had her way, he'd be not the farmer Harry wanted him to be, but some fancy Eastern man with more book sense than common sense. No, he'd taken this drastic measure to ensure his son's future as one of the People. Mythmaker would understand.

He told himself this repeatedly, all the way to the front gate of the doctor's establishment. Dismounting slowly, he straightened his hat, his shirt, wiped his hands on his sleeves. He wished he'd been in his buckskins, his hair braided, wearing his moccasins. Then Mythmaker would have seen the man she'd fallen in love with, that winter he'd found her among the Kiowa. This half-white, half-Comanche he'd been born had become too white, during the years with the Monroes.

Surely, he thought desperately, she must see that. There was no way he could take them back to the free life on the prairie, for it was long gone. But with the ranch, they'd be able to live as they saw fit.

Pausing to knock at the door to the small building behind the doctor's house, he tried to wipe the unhappiness from his eyes. He hated to disagree with his wife, and it rarely happened that he did.

"Mythmaker." He began to speak as the door gave way beneath his next knock.

She faced him, sunk in a wooden chair, her extended legs crossed at the ankles, a wet cloth held to her eyes.

"Sir?" The white man who held the door stared at him as if wondering from what rock he'd crawled under. "Can I help you?"

"I've come for my wife."

Springing up, Mythmaker ran to him with her arms wide. "Johnny!" Without warning, she flung herself at his chest and began to weep.

His first reaction was that the man with his hand still on the doorknob had hurt her. Temper flaring, he turned to stare at the old man.

"What've you done to her?"

"Me?" Laughing, the doctor crossed the room to his rolltop desk and sat heavily before it. "I'd say it's your doing, if you're the lady's husband."

"What?" Johnny stroked Mythmaker's head, patted her back, loath to leave her like this. But every inch of him wanted to pummel the man who had upset her so badly.

"Johnny," Mythmaker said and hiccupped. "I'm fine, really. Just tired, and I didn't realize until now . . . and the doctor confirmed it, and I had no idea, I thought we were lucky to have Whistle, and—"

"Wife," Johnny demanded sternly, "make some sense here. This isn't like you."

The face she turned to him was surprisingly girlish. "No, it's not. But I haven't felt this . . . way, not in about five years."

For a second, he wondered what five years had to do with her tears, then it struck him. Five years ago, he'd left her with her Kiowa friend while he'd searched for the return of the buffalo with the first of the Kiowa prophets to predict their return. She'd been unwell, and later he'd felt guilt at leaving her behind when she'd been in the early stages of expecting Whistle.

"Are you? I mean, will there be another child?"

She nodded, head against his shoulder. "Sorry I'm so weepy. I never do this, Doctor, really." She turned watery eyes to the older man.

"Congratulations, sir, and take care of her. She needs some quiet and rest. Too much excitement by far, for a woman in her condition. Never would have let her assist, if I'd known." He shook some powder from a glass bottle into a piece of paper and folded it carefully. "Give her this, if she's unable to sleep."

Johnny almost laughed at the thought of his wife taking something concocted by a white doctor, she who used herbs to heal everything from colicky cows to sick plants. But the man meant well. Johnny extended his hand to take the folded paper.

"And you, my dear woman, make an excellent nurse. Now go on home with your husband."

Johnny wrapped an arm around her still-slim waist, shook the hand offered by the doctor, and walked his wife to the front gate. He still wasn't able to say anything to her, his throat was too clogged with happiness, gratitude, surprise.

But she straightened herself as soon as they were on the street, tucking stray hairs behind her ears, wiping at her cheeks.

"My goodness, I must look a mess!" She smiled at him happily, as if saying she knew she'd always be beautiful in his eyes. "And I never even asked what you're doing here."

She frowned. "Did something happen to the farm? Fire, hail?"

"No, nothing like that." He looked around, trying to get his bearings to find the livery. "I need to pick up Harry's team, take it to Noble's place."

"You've seen Noble?" Again, she was off-balance. "What happened?" She clutched his hand tightly.

Johnny smiled. "We talked some. That's all."

"What do you mean, that's all? If you don't tell me what's going on, I swear . . ." she warned.

"Let's get the team. I'll have them hitch it to a buggy, so you can drive them. We'll talk then, on the way back." He didn't want to have this discussion in the middle of the street.

Trying to divert her, he asked, "What happened to the man you were helping the doctor sew up? Noble and the sheriff said he was in bad shape."

"Still is. Touch and go with the leg. Worst of it is, I'm not sure he won't get blood poisoning."

"Don't know if anyone told you yet, but the sheriff says he's the one in the Wanted poster. Harry almost got himself killed, and you too, over a man not worth spit." The thought made him so angry, he wanted to shake Harry like a dried cornstalk.

"Doesn't matter. It's over and done with, and we're fine. Harry is, isn't he?"

"Far as I know. We'll see him, I reckon, at Noble's place." He wanted to ride beside her, take the leads, let her lean her head on his shoulder. Maybe then, with the happy glow of a new baby still cocooning them, he'd tell her about the ranch.

They got the team and buggy, and Johnny tied his horse behind. Her long days and short nights had caught up with her, and he saw her eyes fluttering with fatigue. By the time he'd gotten directions from the livery boy, she was half-asleep. The gentle rocking of the buggy did the rest of the job, and he held her up, one hand on the leads, as they rode to Noble's farm.

He had half a mind to keep his mouth shut about

the ranch, and sort it out later. Mythmaker would want Hannah with her when this baby came, and he wasn't about to upset her, not now.

If he had to make a choice, he'd take whatever made his wife happy. He wasn't a stupid man.

Chapter Eighteen

I could barely believe it, when I awoke and found us surrounded by all the people I'd loved who still inhabited this world. *Oh, Grandfather,* I thought silently, *if only you were with us today.* Whistle bounded into his father's arms, then unwrapped one arm from his neck to pull me close and give me a wet kiss. Hannah fluttered, Rebecca shooed us into the house, Johnny and Noble saw to the horses, and Whistle held my hand as though he'd never let it go.

"Rebecca, you're still so pretty." I kissed her cheek, admired her newest girl, about the age of Feather. "I didn't know about this one."

"And we didn't know about Whistle." She laughed gently. "Oh, Sister, it's so good to have you with us again. We've missed you." She spoke softly into my ear. "Hannah and her husband are resting in the back bedroom. They'll be fine."

I squeezed her hand tightly. She'd been my friend when I had none, when Noble had seen me as less than human because I'd loved a half-Comanche. "I've missed you too. And here's a surprise for you."

"Feather!" I couldn't believe my eyes as my Kiowa son enveloped me in a bear hug. "What on earth are you doing here?"

Peck appeared from behind me, giving me a polite nod of the head. "Came to pull my fat from the fire, Mythmaker. Seems he'd decided to face the law with me."

My heart sank. I knew, from the days when Peck hid out with the People, that he was in trouble in the Territory. Magpie had told me the law wanted him for murder.

"Meet my boy, Feather." A small Indian child peeked from behind Peck's leg.

I smiled a greeting at the child, but inside, I was frozen. This couldn't be happening, after so much was going right. I'd watched in amazement as Johnny and Noble had worked in tandem to unhitch the team, chatting casually as they did so. Seeing them together, I almost forgot their years of estrangement.

"Magpie?" I spoke to the boy I'd raised, to the child who'd saved me from a death far worse than the passing of my body from the living. He was a man now, but part of him would always be the little boy I'd prayed over. "Where's Anna? Does she have any say in this plan?"

I knew a woman like Anna Jackson, now Magpie's

wife, would never let him throw his life away on a fool's errand.

Noble and Johnny clattered up the steps of the porch, still chatting as though all was well with the world. For a second, I was annoyed.

"She knows what I have to do."

I could tell from the way he said it that she wasn't in agreement with him. "Magpie, is there any other way? I mean, I know you think Peck's innocent, but do you truly believe . . . ?" I was fumbling for words to ascertain if he was confident of winning the case in a court of law.

"No need for worry." Noble stepped into the crowd in the middle of Rebecca's parlor. I barely noticed the horse-hair sofa or the rosewood table I'd polished often for her.

"Haven't had a chance to tell you, Peck. Sheriff says Gravitt's the man in the poster, all right. Got some information about him too. Seems he's the man they want for that woman's death, down in the Territory. No doubt about it."

I could have sworn Peck turned pale. "You mean it? This isn't some story?"

"I don't make up tales about something like this." Noble was annoyed. "Not in my own home."

Rebecca tried to smooth over the gaffe. "That's wonderful news! You're free, Peck." She turned to me. "How is the man, Mythmaker?"

I was pleased she used the name I'd taken for my own. My brother would probably call me Elizabeth until the day he died, but it no longer bothered me.

"He's alive, but barely. Won't travel for a long time, if he makes it."

"Shoot, forgot about this." Noble reached into his shirt pocket. "Telegraph office said something came in for you, Donaldson."

Peter gulped, then took the sealed envelope from Noble. "Wired my wife I was here. Must be from her." He looked to me like a man with a lot to atone for when he got home.

"All we need is for her to ride up!" Rebecca laughed. "Haven't had this much excitement out here, not since the barn caught fire, oh, three years ago or more!"

"Oh, I don't know about that." Sweeping her into his arms, Noble tried to coax Rebecca into a dance in front of the assembled crowd. "Johnny's got some pretty excitin' news of his own."

I'd slept all the way to the farm. Johnny looked as if he'd rather swallow nails than speak. Before he got a chance, Harry, leaning on Hannah, edged into the room.

"How's a man to sleep with all this racket?" His grin was as wide as his face.

I hurried to hug Hannah, thanking her again for taking care of Whistle when the vigilantes had us dead to rights. "How's he feeling? Bleeding stopped?"

"Doing just fine." Hannah'd lost that haunted look at the edges of her eyes. "Done some talking, and he says he'll go wherever I want, soon as he's up to it. Your sister-in-law invited us to stay as long as we care to, so I think we'll take her up on it. You won't mind, will you, leaving Saint Louis out of our plans for now?''

I could have cried with joy. ''Not one bit. We'll get back to the farm right away, keep it going until you get back.''

''Elizabeth, your husband and I have been talking.'' Noble stepped up beside Hannah, Harry, and me. ''No one's given him a chance to get a word in edgewise, and he's too polite to shout you all down.''

I thought Noble looked awfully pleased with himself. Johnny, however, resembled a man about to be shot by a firing squad.

''Now that Peck here's in the clear, and needs a place to get his bearings, we thought maybe, if it's all right with the Monroes, he'd keep their farm running until they get back. What do you say, Peck?''

I was stunned. Where would we go? The farm had been home to me for so long, I felt adrift without its anchor.

''Johnny? What do you have to say to this?'' Harry was as puzzled as I.

''I'd rather talk to my wife alone.'' Johnny looked grim.

Taking me by the elbow, he steered me outside. I barely noticed where he was leading me as he walked us down the long hill that led to the creek where the blackberries grew. I'd been picking fruit there, when he'd appeared as a silhouette against the sky, not a ghost, but my very much alive husband. Our lives together since then had been a search, although not a constant one, to find our place in this white man's world.

"What's happened? Please, tell me." I knew his way; he'd speak when the words were right in his head, but I was too impatient to wait.

"Came up here with a herd. Ours. Bought it off a man selling out."

I nodded. This would lead somewhere, but he'd demand patience of me. He'd be lucky if I didn't throw up on his feet, I was so nervous.

"Noble's going to help me gentle them, the older ones, find buyers. Going into business together, if you've no objections."

I squeezed his hand tightly. "How could I? But there's more to this plan, isn't there?"

"Yes." He fidgeted a bit, pulled a green berry off a bush, squeezed it between his fingers. "Bought the ranch that went with the horses."

I sat so hard I hit my tailbone. "How're we going to pay for this?" Money had never meant much to Johnny.

"Gave him some, going to pay him monthly. Selling the broke horses from this herd'll give us a leg up."

I wanted to laugh, cry, hiccup, all at the same time. Horses would give him the freedom he craved, the mastery he deserved. He was a man born to this calling.

"Hope Peck can milk a cow, weed the garden." I smiled up at him. "Maybe Rebecca's given him lessons, while he's been here."

Sitting beside me, he waited a second, then gave me a kiss. "If not, I'm sure that between you, Rebecca, and Hannah, he'll be a master at it before he gets to the farm."

I still couldn't believe he was afraid to tell me his news. "Were you really so worried I'd not go with you, to the ranch?"

He shook his head. "No, I know you better than that. But I thought you'd want your say in the matter, beforehand. And now, with this baby coming, you'll want Hannah close by."

"We'll cross that bridge, when we come to it." There was a certain comfort in old clichés. "Harry needs Hannah right now, and she needs him. They'll grow closer, if we aren't there to get in their way."

"Shall we tell them about the baby?" He rubbed the small of my back with his fist, in just the spot that needed kneading.

"Not yet. Let the dust settle first. I wish Hannah had a baby of her own."

"Did you see the way she looked at Peck's little ones?" Johnny chuckled. "I think our son is losing his status with her, rapidly. Show me a child who needs care, and I'll show you Hannah Monroe."

"Good. That boy could use some good, old-fashioned spoiling. Peck won't mind."

"No, I think not. And you, how would you like some old-fashioned spoiling?" Johnny kissed my cheek.

"You can do better than that." I pulled his face to

mine. We were going to be embarrassingly late getting back to the house, but I didn't care about appearances.

Never had, never would.

When we finally got back to the house, dusk had fallen. I hoped I'd dragged all the dry grass out of my hair, but I doubted it. I was a bit embarrassed to find my Magpie sitting on the front steps, all alone, the telegraph wire in his fist.

He didn't see us at first.

"Magpie?" I didn't want to startle him.

The lights from the house spilled out a warm, yellow glow through the opened windows. Cicadas sang their dusky song as voices from inside the house provided a chorus.

"I'm going to be a father." Magpie looked like a steer that had been pole-axed.

"Congratulations!" Johnny shouted.

"I'd say it's about time you went home, don't you?" I patted his shoulder, happy for him, for Anna. Their child would have to learn his way in this white man's world, just as Magpie and Johnny had. I hoped he did half as well.

"Come in to supper, everything's getting cold." Rebecca appeared in the doorway.

"And after that, I'm going home."

I don't think anyone but I heard Magpie's promise to himself.

I knew how he felt. This trail had ended for today,

but there were new ones opening up for us by the minute, by the day.

I took Johnny's arm in my left, Magpie's in my right, and climbed the steps into the warmth of Rebecca's kitchen and the love of family and friends.